ANANDAMATH

ANANDAMATH

A NOVEL BY

BANKIM CHANDRA CHATTERJEE

Translated

SRI AUROBINDO
BARINDRA KUMAR GHOSH

GYAN

Published by

GYAN

Gyan Publishing House
5, Ansari Road
Daryaganj, New Delhi-110002
Phone: 011-47034999, 9811692060
E-mail: books@gyanbooks.com

Distribution Network
gyanbooks.com
India, USA, Canada, UK, Australia

ISBN: 978-93-7414-159-5 (PB)

First Published, 1910

2nd Impression 2025

Printed at: Gyan Press, Delhi.

ANANDAMATH

Translated: SRI AUROBINDO and BARINDRA KUMAR GHOSH

ANANDAMATH

A Novel By
BANKIM CHANDRA CHATTERJEE

<u>Translated from Bengali by</u>

Sri Aurobindo
and
Barindra Kumar Ghosh

Table of Contents

A Note

ANANDAMATH is a reprint of the translation of the Bengali Novel written by Bankim Chandra Chattaijee. It was published by Basumati Sahitya Mandir (166, Bowbazar Street, Calcutta) with a note "up to 15th chapter of Part I translated by Sree Aurobindo. Subsequent pages translated by Sree Barindra Kumar Ghosh." Year of publication was not printed on this edition.

According to SABCL (Sri Aurobindo Birth Centenary Library), Vol. 30 'The prologue and the first thirteen chapters of Part I were translated by Sri Aurobindo, the rest by his brother Barindra. The parts translated by Sri Aurobindo first appeared in the KARMAYOGIN, intermittently between August 7, 1909 and February 12, 1910."

Foreword

Sree Aurobindo returned from England to India on or about February, 1893. He had been in England for 14 years (1879-93). He was taken to England when he was only seven years old. After returning to India, Aurobindo wrote several series of articles: "New Lamps for Old", in the *Indu Prakash*, from August 7, 1893 till March, 1894.

Bankim died on April 8, 1894.

So, the first year of Aurobindo after his return to India was the last year of Bankim's life.

In the series "New Lamps for Old" Aurobindo devoted himself to attack the "medicant policy" of the Congress. He also attacked the "bourgeois" politics of the Congress and advocated the uplift of the "proletariate": he introduced a socialist programme. He also suggested that like the French Revolution, unless there is a "purification by blood and fire", the nation will not get the desired end — Freedom.

Aurobindo's criticism had its effect not so much upon the Government itself, as on the Bombay moderates. Mr. Justice Ranade had Aurobindo called before him and asked him to discontinue his attack on the Congress. Aurobindo had been carrying on the attack for eight months and he acceded to Mr. Ranade's request and gave up writing against the Congress (March, 1894). In the next month, Bankim died (April 8, 1894).

About three months after Bankim's death Aurobindo wrote in the *Indu Prakash* seven articles on Bankim Chandra Chatterji (July 16 – August 27, 1894). This serial of the seven articles on Bankim was a discovery made for me by the Hon'ble Justice Mr. K. C. Sen of the Bombay High Court in 1940-41. The articles were: "Youth to College Life" (July 16); "The Bengal he lived in", (July 23); "His Official Career" (July, 30); "His versatility" (August, 6); "His literary history" (August 13); "What he did for Bengal" (August 20) and "Our hope in the future" (August 27); three articles in July; four in August, 1894. These articles clearly prove that Bankim had a great influence on Aurobindo. Let me quote a few passages from these articles:

"More difficulties enter into any, comparison of him (Bankim) with the best English novelists; yet I think he stands higher than any of them, except one; in certain qualities of each he may fall short, but his sum of qualities is greater; and he has this supreme advantage over that he is a more faultless artist. In his life and fortunes, and sometimes even in his character, he bears a striking resemblance to the father of English fiction, Henry Fielding; but the literary work of the two men moves upon different planes. Philosophical culture and deep feeling for the poetry of life and unfailing sense of beauty are distinguishing marks of Bankim's style; they find no place in Fielding's. Again, Bankim, after a rather silly fashion of speaking now greatly in vogue, has been pointed out by some as the Scott of Bengal. It is a marvellous thing that the people who misuse this phrase as an encomium, cannot understand that it conveys an insult. They would have us imagine that one of the most perfect and original of novelists is a mere replica of a faulty and incomplete Scotch author! Scott had many marvellous and unique gifts, but his defects are at least as striking. His style is never quite sure; indeed, except in his inspired moments, he has no style: his Scotch want of humour is always militating against his power of vivid incident; his characters, and chiefly those in whom he should interest us most, are usually very manifest puppets; and they have all this shortcoming, that they have no soul; they may be splendid or striking or bold creations, but they live from outside and not from within. Scott could paint outlines, but he could not fill them in. Here Bankim excels; speech and action with him are so closely interpenetrated and suffused with a deeper existence that his characters give us the sense of their being real men and women. Moreover to the wonderful passion and poetry of his finest reactions there are in English fiction, outside the Brontes and the supreme genius, George Meredith, no parallel instances. Insight into the secret of his feminine characters, that is another notable concomittant of the best dramatic power and that too Bankim possesses. Wade as you will through the bog of contemporary fiction, you, will meet no living woman there. Even the novelists of genius stop short at the outside; they cannot find their way into the soul. Here again Fielding fails us; Scott's women are a mere gallery of wax figures, Rebecca herself being no more than a highly coloured puppet; even in Thackeray, the real women are three or four. But the supreme dramatic genius has found out this secret of feminity.

Shakespear had it to any degree, and in our country, Meredith, and among, ourselves Bankim. The social reformer, gazing, of course through that admirable pair of spectacles given to him by the Calcutta University, can find nothing excellent in Hindu life, except its cheapness, or in Hindu Woman, except her subserviency. Beyond this he only sees its narrowness and her ignorance. But Bankim had the eye of a poet and saw much deeper than this. He saw what was beautiful and sweet and gracious in Hindu life, and what was lovely and noble in Hindu woman, her deep heart of emotion, her steadfastness, tenderness and lovableness, in fact, her woman's souls and all this we find burning in his pages and made diviner by the touch of a poet and an artist. Our social reformers might learn something from Bankim. Their zeal at present is too little ruled by discretion. They are like bad tailors, very clever at spoiling the rich stuff given over to their shaping but quite unable to fit the necessities of the future. They have passed woman through an English crucible and in the place of the old type which, with all its fatal defects, had in it some supreme possibilities, they have turned out a soulless and superficial being fit only for flirtation, matchmaking and playing on the piano. They seem to have a passion for reforming every good thing out of existence. It is about time that this miserable bungling should stop. Surely it would be possible, without spoiling that divine nobleness of soul to give it a wider culture and mightier channels. So we should have a race of women intellectually as well as emotionally noble, fit to be the mothers not of chatterers and money-makers but of high thinkers and heroic doers.

Of Bankim's style I shall hardly trust myself to speak. To describe its beauty, terseness, strength and sweetness is too high a task for a pen like mine. I will remark this only that what marks Bankim above all, is his unfailing sense of beauty. This is indeed the note of Bengali literature and the one thing that it has gained from close acquaintance with European models. The hideous grotesques of old Hindu Art, the monkey rabble of Ram and the ten heads of Ravan are henceforth impossible to it. The *Shakuntala* itself is not governed by a more perfect graciousness of conception or diffused with a more human sweetness than *Kopal Kundala* and the *Poison Tree*"

— Bankim Chandra Chatterji: His Literary History;

"Indu Prakash", August 23, 1894.

Aurobindo, when he wrote this; was only twenty two years old. Apart from his premature conception of Hindu Art, this is his first admiration of Bankim in the first year after the latter's death. He compares Bankim with the best novelists in English literature and finds him much above them. He also compares Bankim with even Kalidas and calls Bankim a "faultless artist". About Bankim's character Aurobindo writes:

"He (Bankim) had been a sensuous youth and a joyous man. Gifted supremely with the artist's sense for the warmth and beauty of life, he had turned with a smile from the savage austerities of the ascetic and with a shudder from the dreary creed of the puritan."

—Ibid: August 13, 1894.

Like his elder brother. Professor Manmohan Ghose, Aurobindo is a poet of great eminence. He wrote a poem on Bankim, — "Saraswati with the Lotus" — in the same year; 1894. Shortly after, he wrote another poem, — "Bankim Chandra Chatteiji" — characterising him as "The sweetest voice that ever spoke in prose".

In 1898 Aurobindo took a regular course of study of Bengali literature under Dinendra Kumar Roy who has written that Aurobindo used to read Bankim without any help and clearly understood it.

In 1905 Aurobindo wrote "Bhabani Mandir", while at Baroda. It was a political pamphlet with a revolutionary purpose. He got it printed and distributed in Calcutta by his younger brother, Barindra Kumar Ghose. The Rowlatt Committee did not know, even in 1918, that Aurobindo was the author of this pamphlet. In this pamphlet Aurobindo has laboured under direct influence of Bankim's novel, *Anandamath.*

"It will be remembered that in 1906 was published the pamphlet Bhawani Mandir, which set out the aims and objects of the revolutionaries. It was remarkable in more ways than one.... The central idea as to a given religious order is taken from the well-known novel "Anandamath" of Bankim Chandra. It is an historical novel, having for its setting the Sanyasi rebellion of 1774, when armed bands of Sanyasis came into conflict with the East India Company and were suppressed after a temporary career of success...

The revolutionary societies in Bengal infected the principles and rules advocated in the Bhawani Mandir with the Russian ideas of revolutionary violence. While a great deal is said in the Bhawani Mandir about the religious aspect, the Russian rules are matter of fact. The samitis and associations formed later than 1908 gradually dropped the religious ideas underlying the Bhawani Mandir pamphlet (with the exception of the formalities of oaths and vows) and developed the terroristic aide with its necessary accompaniments of dacoity and murder."

— Rowlatt Committee Report.

In *Bhawani Mandir* (1905) we find Aurobindo under the direct influence of *Ananda Math.* This influence is not literary so much as political with the "Russian ideas of revolutionary violence". More than one political disciple of Aurobindo, particularly Hem Chandra Kanungo, have already admitted that they wanted to put *Ananda Math* into action in their attempts at secret murders during 1906, '07, '08, under the leadership of Aurobindo.

"Aurobindo was not only the leader and prophet of an open national movements but also the demi-god and, creator of an underground movement too. It may be a surprise for India to know this startling fact, but it is no news to the Government of India who pursued him at one time relentlessly until Sri Aurobindo had to escape out of British India.... Apart from his annual Puja visits, he came twice to Bengal with special mission which ought to be recorded in history as having deep and revolutionary significance."

— "Dawn of India," 15th Dec, 1933;
Barindra Kumar Ghose

With this clear admission by the two direct disciples of Aurobindo, one can easily understand what use Aurobindo made of *Ananda Math* in his early career of political activities. *Ananda Math* had a special significance for Aurobindo.

In 1907 (16th April) Aurobindo wrote "Rishi Bankim" in *Bande Mataram.* It was later reprinted as a pamphlet with the English translation in prose of the "Bande Mataram" song. Aurobindo wrote:

"The Rishi is different from the Saint. His life may not have been distinguished by superior holiness nor his character by an ideal beauty. He is not great by what he was himself, but by what he has expressed."

— *Rishi Bankim.*

I cannot say definitely if Aurobindo in his idea of "Rishi Bankim" (describing the Rishi as not the same thing as a Saint) deliberately gave an answer to the attack made by Pandit Sivanath Sastri on Bankim's character in "Ramtanu Lahiri-O-Tatkalin-Banga-Samaj."

"He, first of our great publicists, understood the hollowness and inutility of the methods of political agitation — which prevailed in his time and exposed it with merciless satire in his "Lokrahasya" and "Kamala Kanta's Daftar"... He bade us leave the canine methods of agitation for the leonine. The Mother of his vision held trenchant steel in her twice seventy million hands and not the bowl of the mendicant...

In "Anandamath" this idea (work for one's country and one's kind) is the keynote of the whole book and received its perfect lyrical expression in the great song which has become the national anthem of United India.... It was thirty-two years ago that Bankim wrote his great song and few listened; but in a sudden movement of awakening from long delusions the people of Bengal looked round for the truth and in a fated moment somebody sang *Bande Mataram.* The *mantram* had been given and in a single day a whole people had been converted to the religion of patriotism."

— *Rishi Bankim.*

The *Anand Math* was first published in 1883, twenty-six year (and not thirty, as said above) before Aurobindo wrote "Rishi Bankim".

In 1894 Aurobindo found Bankim as "faultless artist"; in 1907, he discovers in him a political *Guru* and this is due mainly to the influence of *Ananda Math* and the *Bande Mataram* song on Aurobindo. In 1908 (29th, January) Aurobindo delivered a speech at Amraoti (Berar). In this speech:

The song, he said, was not only a National anthem as the European nations looked upon their own, but one replete with mighty power, being a sacred 'mantra' revealed to us by the author of "Ananda math" who might be called an inspired "Rishi"... The "mantra" of Bankim Chandra was not appreciated in his own day, and he predicted that there would come a time when the whole of India would resound with the singing of the song, and the word of the prophet was miraculously fulfilled."

Aurobindo was arrested on the 2nd May 1908, in connection with the now famous Alipore Bomb Case. He was detained in jail for full one year. Mr. C. R. Das, a friend of Aurobindo and the greatest lawyer of state-trials in India, defended him successfully. Aurobindo was released on May 6, 1909. Only 3½ months after his release, Aurobindo started this English translation of *Ananda Math* in the *Karmayogin,* from August 14, 1909; and he finished up to the 15th chapter of Part I of the book.

In translating *Ananda Math* what other motive he had, over and above the literary interest, is rather difficult to guess. But the chronology proves that Aurobindo first attempted to translate *Ananda Math* into action and subsequently failing therein, he attempted to translate it into English for a wider public. But as he did not find time during these long years to complete his translation, one may doubt if he at present has the same interest in the book itself as he certainly had when he started the translation.

Girija Sankar Roy Chaudhuri

Prologue

A wide interminable forest. Most of the trees are *sals*, but other kinds are not wanting. Treetop mingling with treetop, foliage melting into foliage, the interminable lines progress; without crevice, without gap, without even a way for the light to enter, league after league and again league after league the boundless ocean of leaves advances, tossing wave upon wave in the wind. Underneath, thick darkness; even at midday the light is dim and uncertain; a seat of terrific gloom. There the foot of man never treads; there except the illimitable rustle of the leaves and the cry of wild beasts and birds, no sound is heard.

In this interminable, impenetrable wilderness of blind gloom, it is night. The hour is midnight and a very dark midnight; even outside the woodland it is dark and nothing can be seen. Within the forest the piles of gloom are like the darkness in the womb of the earth itself.

Bird and beast are utterly and motionlessly still. What hundreds of thousands, what millions of birds, beasts, insects, flying things have their dwelling within that forest, but not one is giving forth a sound. Rather the darkness is within the imagination, but inconceivable is that noiseless stillness of the ever-murmurous, ever noise-filled earth. In that limitless empty forest, in the solid darkness of that midnight, in that unimaginable silence there was a sound, "Shall the desire of my heart ever be fulfilled?"

After that sound the forest reaches sank again into stillness. Who would have said then that a human sound had been heard in those wilds? A little while after, the sound came again, again the voice of man rang forth troubling the hush, "Shall the desire of my heart ever be fulfilled?"

Three times the wide sea of darkness was thus shaken. Then the answer came, "What is the stake put down?"

The first voice replied, "I have staked my life and all its riches."

The echo answered, "Life! it is a small thing which all can sacrifice."

"What else is there? What more can I give?"

This was the answer, "Thy soul's worship."

PART I

Chapter I

IT was a summer day of the Bengali year 1176. The glare and heat of the sun lay very heavy on the village of Padachinha. The village wa*s* *crow*ded with houses, yet there was no*t a ma*n to be seen. Line upon *line* of shops in the bazaar, row upon row of booths in the mart, hundreds of earthen houses interspersed with stone mansions high and low in every quarter. But today all was silent. In the bazaar the shops are closed, and where the shopkeeper has fled no man can tell. It is market day today, but in the mart there is no buying and selling. It is the beggars' day but the beggars are not out. The weaver has shut up his loom and lies weeping in his house; the trader has forgotten his traffic and weeps with his infant in his lap; the givers have left giving and the teachers closed their schools; the very infant, it would seem, has no longer heart to cry aloud. No wayfarers are to be seen in the highways, no bathers in the lake, no human forms at door and threshold, no birds in the trees, no cattle in the pastures, only in the burning-ground dog and jackal crowd. In that crowded desolation of houses one huge building whose great fluted pillars could be seen from afar, rose glorious as the peak of a hill. And yet where was the glory? The doors were shut, the house empty of the concourse of men, hushed and voiceless, difficult even to the entry of the wind. In a room within this dwelling where even noon was a darkness, in that darkness, like a pair of lilies flowering in the midnight, a wedded couple sat in thought. Straight in front of them stood Famine.

The harvest of the year 1174 had been poor, consequently in the year 1175 rice was a little dear; the people suffered, but the Government exacted its revenues to the last fraction of a farthing. As a result of this careful reckoning the poor began to eat only once a day. The rains in 1175 were copious and people thought Heaven had taken pity on the land. Joyously once more the herdsman sang his ditty in the fields, the tiller's wife again began to tease her husband for a silver bracelet. Suddenly in the month of Aswin Heaven turned away its face. In Aswin and Kartik not a drop of rain fell; the grain in the fields withered and turned to straw as it stood. Wherever an ear or two flourished, the officials bought it for the troops. The people no longer had anything to eat. First they stinted themselves of one meal in the day, then even from their single meal they rose with half-filled stomachs, next the two meal-times became two fasts. The little harvest reaped in Chaitra was not enough to fill the hungry mouths. But Mahomed Reza Khan, who was in charge of the revenues, thought fit to show himself off as a loyal servant and immediately enhanced the taxes by ten per cent. Throughout Bengal arose a clamour of great weeping.

First, people began to live by begging, but afterwards who could give alms? They began to fast. Next they fell into the clutch of disease. The cow was sold, plough and yoke were sold, the seed-rice was eaten, hearth and home were sold, land and goods were sold. Next they began to sell their girls. After that they began to sell their boys. After that they began to sell their wives. Next girl, boy, or wife, — who would buy? Purchasers there were none, only sellers. For want of food men began to eat the leaves of trees, they began to eat grass, they began to eat weeds. The lower castes and the forest men began devouring dogs, mice and cats. Many fled, but those who fled only reached some foreign land to die of starvation. Those who remained ate uneatables or subsisted without food till disease took hold of them and they died.

Disease had its day, — fever, cholera, consumption, smallpox. The virulence of smallpox was especially great. In every house men began to perish of the disease. There was none to give water to his fellow, none who would touch him, none to treat the sick. Men would not turn to care for each other's sufferings, nor was there any to take up the corpse from where it lay. Beautiful bodies lay rotting in wealthy mansions. For where once the smallpox made its entry, the dwellers fled from the house and abandoned the sick man in their fear.

Mohendra Singha was a man of great wealth in the village of Padchinha, but today rich and poor were on one level. In this time of crowding afflictions his relatives, friends, servants, maidservants had all been seized by disease and gone from him. Some had died, some had fled. In that once peopled household there was only himself, his wife and one infant girl. This was the couple of whom I spoke.

The wife, Kalyani, gave up thinking and went to the cowshed to milk the cow; then she warmed the milk, fed her child and went again to give the cow its grass and water. When she returned from her task Mohendra said, “How long can we go on in this way?”

“Not long;” answered Kalyani, “as long as we can. So long as possible I will keep things going, afterwards you and the girl can go to the town.”

Mohendra: “If we have to go to the town at the end, why should I inflict all this trouble on you at all? Come, let us go at once.”

After much arguing and contention between husband and wife, Kalyani said, “Will there be any particular advantage in going to the town?”

Mohendra: “Very possibly that place too is as empty of men and empty of means of subsistence as we are here.”

Kalyani: “If you go to Murshidabad, Cassimbazar or Calcutta, you may save your life. It is in every way best to leave this place.”

Mohendra answered, “This house has been full for many years of the gathered wealth of generations. All this will be looted by thieves!”

Kalyani: “If thieves come to loot it, shall we two be able to protect the treasure? If life is not saved who will be there to enjoy? Come, let us shut up the whole place this moment and go. If we survive, we can come back and enjoy what remains.”

“Will you be able to do the journey on foot?” asked Mohendra. “The palanquin-bearers are all dead. As for cart or carriage, where there are bullocks there is no driver and where there is a driver there are no bullocks.”

Kalyani: “Oh, I shall be able to walk, do not fear.”

In her heart she thought, even if she fell and died on the way, these two at least would be saved.

The next day at dawn the two took some money with them, locked up room and door, let loose the cattle, took the child in their arms and set out for the capital. At the time of starting Mohendra said, “The road is very difficult, at every step dacoits and highwaymen are hovering about, it is not well to go empty-handed.” So saying Mohendra returned to the house and took from it musket, shot, and powder.

When she saw the weapon, Kalyani said, “Since you have

remembered to take arms with you, hold Sukumari for a moment and I too will bring a weapon with me." With the words she put her daughter into Mohendra's arms and in her turn entered the house.

Mohendra called after her, "Why, what weapon can you take with you?"

As she came, Kalyani hid a small casket of poison in her dress. Fearing what fate might befall her in these days of misfortune, she had already procured and kept the poison with her.

It was the month of Jyaistha, a savage heat, the earth as if aflame, the wind scattering fire, the sky like a canopy of heated copper, the dust of the road like sparks of fire. Kalyani began to perspire profusely. Now resting under the shade of a babla-tree, now sitting in the shelter of a date-palm, drinking the muddy water of dried ponds, with great difficulty she journeyed forward. The girl was in Mohendra's arms and sometimes he fanned her with his robe. Once the two refreshed themselves, seated under the boughs of a creeper-covered tree flowering with odorous blooms and dark-hued with dense shade-giving foliage. Mohendra wondered to see Kalyani's endurance under fatigue. He drenched his robe with water from a neighbouring pool and sprinkled it on his and Kalyani's face, forehead, hands and feet.

Kalyani was a little cooled and refreshed, but both of them were distressed with great hunger. That could be borne, but the hunger and thirst of their child could not be endured, so they resumed their march. Swimming through those waves of fire they arrived before evening at an inn. Mohendra had cherished a great hope that on reaching the inn he would be able to give cool water to his wife and child to drink and food to save their lives. But he met with a great disappointment. There was not a man in the inn. Big rooms were lying empty, the men had all fled. Mohendra after looking about the place made his wife and daughter lie down in one of the rooms. He began to call from outside in a loud voice, but got no answer. Then Mohendra said to Kalyani, "Will you have a little courage and stay here alone? If there is a cow to be found in this region, may Sri Krishna have pity on us and I shall bring you some milk." He took an earthen water jar in his hand and went out. A number of such jars were lying about the place.

Chapter II

MOHENDRA departed. Left alone with no one near her but a little girl, Kalyani in that solitary and unpeopled place, in that almost pitch-dark cottage began to study closely every side. Great fear was upon her. No one anywhere, no sound of human existence to be heard, only the howling of the dogs and the jackals. She regretted letting her husband go, — hunger and thirst might after all have been borne a little longer. She thought of shutting all the doors and sitting in the security of the closed house. But not a single door had either panel or bolt. As she was thus gazing in every direction suddenly something in the doorway that faced her caught her eye, something like a shadow. It seemed to her to have the shape of a man and yet not to be human. Something utterly dried up and withered, something like a very black, a naked and terrifying human shape had come and was standing at the door. After a little while the shadow seemed to lift a hand, — with the long withered finger of a long withered hand, all skin and bone, it seemed to make a motion of summons to someone outside. Kalyani's heart dried up in her with fear. Then just such another shadow, withered, black, tall, naked, came and stood by the side of the first. Then another came and yet another came. Many came, — slowly, noiselessly they began to enter the room. The room with its almost blind darkness grew dreadful as a midnight burning-ground. All those corpselike figures gathered round Kalyani and her daughter. Kalyani almost swooned away. Then the black withered men seized and lifted up the woman and the girl, carried them out of the house and entered into a jungle across the open fields.

A few minutes afterwards Mohendra arrived with the milk in the water jar. He found the whole place empty. Hither and thither he searched, often called aloud his daughter's name and at last even his wife's. There was no answer, he could find no trace of his wife and child.

Chapter III

IT was a very beautiful woodland in which the robbers set down Kalyani. There was no light, no eye to see the loveliness, — the beauty of the wood remained invisible like the beauty of soul in a poor man's heart. There might be no food in the country, but there was wealth of flowers in the woodland; so thick was the fragrance that even in that darkness one seemed to be conscious of a light. On a clear spot in the middle covered with soft grass the thieves set down Kalyani and her child and themselves sat around them. Then they began to debate what to do with them, for what ornaments Kalyani had with her were already in their possession. One group was very busy with the division of this booty. But when the ornaments had been divided, one of the robbers said, "What are we to do with gold and silver? Someone give me a handful of rice in exchange for an ornament; I am tortured with hunger, I have eaten today nothing but the leaves of trees." No sooner had one so spoken than all echoed him and a clamour arose. "Give us rice, give us rice, we do not want gold and silver!" The leader tried to quiet them, but no one listened to him. Gradually high words began to be exchanged, abuse flowed freely, a fight became imminent. Everyone in a rage pelted the leader with his whole allotment of ornaments. He also struck one or two and this brought all of them upon him striking at him in a general assault. The robber captain was emaciated and ill with starvation, one or two blows laid him prostrate and lifeless. Then one in that hungry, wrathful, excited, maddened troop of plunderers cried out, "We have eaten the flesh of dogs and jackals and now we are racked with hunger; come, friends, let us feast today on this rascal." Then all began to shout aloud "Glory to Kali! Bom Kali!! today we will eat human flesh." And with this cry those black emaciated corpselike figures began to shout with laughter and dance and clap their hands in the congenial darkness. One of them set about lighting a fire to roast the body of the leader. He gathered dried creepers, wood and grass, struck flint and iron and set light to the collected fuel. As the fire burned up a little, the dark green foliage of the trees that were neighbours to the spot, mango, lemon, jackfruit and palm, tamarind and date, were lit up faintly with the flames.

Here the leaves seemed ablaze, there the grass brightened in the light; in some places the darkness only became more crass and deep. When the fire was ready, one began to drag the corpse by the leg and was about to throw it on the fire, but another intervened and said "Drop it! stop, stop! if it is on the grand meat that we must keep ourselves alive today, then why the tough and juiceless flesh of this old fellow? We shall eat what we have looted and brought with us today. Come along, there is that tender girl, let us roast and eat her." Another said "Roast anything you like, my good fellow, but roast it; I can stand this hunger no longer." Then all gazed greedily towards the place where Kalyani and her daughter had lain. They saw the place empty; neither child nor mother was there. Kalyani had seen her opportunity when the robbers were disputing, taken her daughter into her arms, put the child's mouth to her breast and fled into the wood. Aware of the escape of their prey, the ghostlike ruffian crew ran in every direction with a cry of "Kill, kill". In certain conditions man is no better than a ferocious wild beast.

Chapter IV

THE darkness of the wood was very deep and Kalyani could not find her way. In the thickly-woven entanglement of trees, creepers and thorns there was no path at the best of times and on that there came this impenetrable darkness. Separating the branches and creepers, pushing through thorn and briar Kalyani began to make her way into the thickness of the wood. The thorns pierced the child's skin and she cried from time to time; and at that the shouts of the pursuing robbers rose higher. In this way with torn and bleeding body, Kalyani made far progress into the woodland. After a little while the moon rose. Until then there was some slight confidence in Kalyani's mind that in the darkness the robbers would not be able to find her and after a brief and fruitless search would desist from the pursuit, but, now that the moon had risen, that confidence left her. The moon, as it mounted into the sky, shed its light on the woodland tops and the darkness within was suffused with it. The darkness brightened, and here and there, through gaps, the outer luminousness found its way inside and peeped into the thickets. The higher the moon mounted, the more the light penetrated into the reaches of foliage, the deeper all the shadows took refuge in the thicker parts of the forest. Kalyani too with her child hid herself farther and farther in where the shadows retreated. And now the robbers shouted higher and began to come running from all sides, and the child in her terror wept louder. Kalyani then gave up the struggle and made no farther attempt to escape. She sat down with the girl on her lap on a grassy thornless spot at the foot of a great tree and called repeatedly "Where art Thou? Thou whom I worship daily, to whom daily I bow down, in reliance on whom I had the strength to penetrate into this forest, where art Thou, O Madhusudan?" At this time, what with fear, the deep emotion of spiritual love and worship and the lassitude of hunger and thirst, Kalyani gradually lost sense of her outward surroundings and became full of an inward consciousness in which she was aware of a heavenly voice singing in mid-air,

"O Hari, O Murari, O foe of Kaitabh and Madhu!
O Gopal, O Govinda, O Mukunda, O Shauri!
O Hari, O Murari, O foe of Kaitabh and Madhu!"

Kalyani had heard from her childhood, in the recitation of the Puranas, that the sages of Paradise roam the world on the paths of the sky, crying aloud to the music of the harp the name of Hari. That imagination took shape in her mind and she began to see with the inner vision a mighty ascetic, harp in hand, whitebodied, whitehaired, whitebearded, whiterobed, tall of stature, singing in the path of the azure heavens,

"O Hari, O Murari, O foe of Kaitabh and Madhu!"

Gradually the song grew nearer, louder she heard the words,

"O Hari, O Murari, O foe of Kaitabh and Madhu!"

Then still nearer, still clearer,

"O Hari, O Murari, O foe of Kaitabh and Madhu!"

At last over Kalyani's head the chant rang echoing in the wood-land,

"O Hari, O Murari, O foe of Kaitabh and Madhu!"

Then Kalyani opened her eyes. In the half-lustrous moonbeams suffused and shadowed with the darkness of the forest, she saw in front of her that whitebodied, whitehaired, whitebearded, whiterobed image of a sage. Dreamily all her consciousness centred on the vision. Kalyani thought to bow down to it, but she could not perform the salutation; even as she bent her head, all consciousness left her and she lay fallen supine on the ground.

Chapter V

IN a huge tract of ground in the forest there was a great monastery engirt with ruined masses of stone. Archaeologists would tell us that this was formerly a monastic retreat of the Buddhists and afterwards became a Hindu monastery. Its rows of edifices were two-storeyed; in between were temples and in front a meeting-hall. Almost all these buildings were surrounded with a wall and so densely hidden with the trees of the forest that, even at daytime and at a short distance from the place, none could divine the presence of a human habitation here. The buildings were broken in many places, but by daylight one could see that the whole place had been recently repaired. A glance showed that man had made his dwelling in this profound and inaccessible wilderness. It was in a room in this monastery, where a great log was blazing, that Kalyani first returned to consciousness and beheld in front of her that whitebodied, whiterobed Great One. Kalyani began once more to gaze on him with eyes large with wonder, for even now memory did not return to her. Then the Mighty One of Kalyani's vision spoke to her, "My child, this is a habitation of the Gods, here have no apprehension. I have a little milk, drink it and then I will talk with you."

At first Kalyani could understand nothing, then, as by degrees her mind recovered some firm foundation, she threw the hem of her robe round her neck and made an obeisance at the Great One's feet. He replied with a blessing and brought out from another room a sweet-smelling earthen pot in which he warmed some milk at the blazing fire. When the milk was warm he gave it to Kalyani and said, "My child, give some to your daughter to drink and then drink some yourself, afterwards you can talk." Kalyani, with joy in her heart, began to administer the milk to her daughter. The unknown then said to her, "While I am absent, have no anxiety," and left the temple. After a while he returned from outside and saw that Kalyani had finished giving the milk to her child, but had herself drunk nothing; the milk was almost as it was at first, very little had been used. "My child," said the unknown, "you have not drunk the milk; I am going out again, and until you drink I will not return."

The sage-like personage was again leaving the room, when Kalyani once more made him an obeisance and stood before him with folded hands.

"What is it you wish to say?" asked the recluse.

Then Kalyani replied, "Do not command me to drink the milk, there is an obstacle. I will not drink it."

The recluse answered in a voice full of compassion, "Tell me what is the obstacle; I am a forest-dwelling ascetic, you are my daughter; what can you have to say which you will not tell me? When I carried you unconscious from the forest, you then seemed to me as if you had been sadly distressed with thirst and hunger; if you do not eat and drink, how can you live?"

Kalyani answered, the tears dropping from her eyes, "You are a god and I will tell you. My husband remains still fasting and until I meet him again or hear of his tasting food, how can I eat?"

The ascetic asked, "Where is your husband?"

"I do not know," said Kalyani, "the robbers stole me away after he had gone out in search of milk." Then the ascetic by question after question elicited all the information about Kalyani and her husband. Kalyani did not indeed utter her husband's name, — she could not; but the other information the ascetic received about him was sufficient for him to understand. He asked her, "Then you are Mohendra Singha's wife?" Kalyani, in silence and with bowed head, began to heap wood on the fire at which the milk had been warmed. Then the ascetic said, "Do what I tell you, drink the milk; I am bringing you news of your husband. Unless you drink the milk, I will not go." Kalyani asked, "Is there a little water anywhere here?" The ascetic pointed to a jar of water. Kalyani made a cup of her hands, the ascetic filled it with water; then Kalyani, approaching her hands with the water in them to the ascetic's feet, said "Please put the dust of your feet in the water." When the ascetic had touched the water with his foot, Kalyani drank it and said, "I have drunk nectar of the gods, do not tell me to eat or drink anything else; until I have news of my husband I will take nothing else." The ascetic answered, "Abide without fear in this temple. I am going in search of your husband."

Chapter VI

IT was far on in the night and the moon rode high overhead. It was not the full moon and its brilliance was not so keen. An uncertain light, confused with shadowy hints of darkness, lay over an open common of immense extent, the two extremities of which could not be seen in that pale lustre. This plain affected the mind like something illimitable and desert, a very abode of fear. Through it there ran the road between Murshidabad and Calcutta.

On the road-side was a small hill which bore upon it a goodly number of mango-trees. The tree-tops glimmered and trembled with a sibilant rustle in the moonlight, and their shadows too, black upon the blackness of the rocks, shook and quivered. The ascetic climbed to the top of the hill and there in rigid silence listened, but for what he listened, it is not easy to say; for, in that great plain that seemed as vast as infinity, there was not a sound except the murmurous rustle of the trees. At one spot there is a great jungle near the foot of the hill, — the hill above, the high road below, the jungle between. I do not know what sound met his ear from the jungle, but it was in that direction the ascetic went. Entering into the denseness of the growth he saw in the forest, under the darkness of the branches at the foot of long rows of trees, men sitting, — men tall of stature, black of hue, armed; their burnished weapons glittered fierily in the moonlight where it fell through gaps in the woodland leafage. Two hundred such armed men were sitting there, not one uttering a single word. The ascetic went slowly into their midst and made some signal, but not a man rose, none spoke, none made a sound. He passed in front of all, looking at each as he went, scanning every face in the gloom, as if he were seeking someone he could not find. In his search he recognised one, touched him and made a sign, at which the other instantly rose. The ascetic took him to a distance and they stood and talked apart. The man was young; his handsome face wore a thick black moustache and beard; his frame was full of strength; his whole presence beautiful and attractive. He wore an ochre-coloured robe and on all his limbs the fairness and sweetness of sandal was smeared. The Brahmacharin said to him, "Bhavananda, have you any news of Mohendra Singha?"

Bhavananda answered, "Mohendra Singha and his wife and child left their house today; on the way, at the inn — "

At this point the ascetic interrupted him, "I know what happened at the inn. Who did it?"

"Village rustics, I imagine. Just now the peasants of all the villages have turned dacoits from compulsion of hunger. And who is not a dacoit nowadays? Today we also have looted and eaten. Two maunds of rice belonging to the Chief of Police were on its way; we took and consecrated it to a devotee's dinner."

The ascetic laughed and said, "I have rescued his wife and child from the thieves. I have just left them in the monastery. Now it is your charge to find out Mohendra and deliver his wife and daughter into his keeping. Jivananda's presence here will be sufficient for the success of today's business."

Bhavananda undertook the mission and the ascetic departed elsewhere.

Chapter VII

MOHENDRA rose from the floor of the inn where he was sitting, for nothing could be gained by sitting there and thinking over his loss. He started in the direction of the town with the idea of taking the help of the officials in the search for his wife and child. After journeying for some distance he saw in the road a number of bullock-carts surrounded by a great company of sepoys.

In the Bengali year 1175 the province of Bengal had not become subject to British administration. The English were then the revenue officials of Bengal. They collected the taxes due to the treasury, but up to that time they had not taken upon themselves the burden of protecting the life and property of the Bengali people. The burden they had accepted was to take the country's money; the responsibility of protecting life and property lay upon that despicable traitor and disgrace to humanity, Mirzafar. Mirzafar was incapable of protecting even himself; it was not likely that he would or could protect the people of Bengal. Mirzafar took opium and slept; the English raked in the rupees and wrote despatches; as for the people of Bengal they wept and went to destruction.

The taxes of the province were therefore the due of the English, but the burden of administration was on the Nawab. Wherever the English themselves collected the taxes due to them, they had appointed a collector, but the revenue collected went to Calcutta. People might die of starvation, but the collection of their monies did not stop for a moment. However, very much could not be collected; for if Mother Earth does not yield wealth, no one can create wealth out of nothing. Be that as it may, the little that could be collected, had been made into cartloads and was on its way to the Company's treasury at Calcutta in charge of a military escort. At this time there was great danger from dacoits, so fifty armed sepoys marched with fixed bayonets, ranked before and behind the carts. Their captain was an English soldier who went on horseback in the rear of the force. On account of the heat the sepoys did not march by day but only by night. As they marched, Mohendra's progress was stopped by the treasure carts and this military array. Mohendra, seeing his way barred by sepoys and carts, stood at the side of the road; but as the sepoys still jostled him in passing, holding this to be no fit time for debate, he went and stood at the edge of the jungle by the road.

Then a sepoy said in Hindustani, "See, there's a dacoit making off." The sight of the gun in Mohendra's hand confirmed this belief. He went for Mohendra, caught hold of his neck and, with the salutation "Rogue! thief!" suddenly gave him a blow of the fist and wrested the gun from his hand. Mohendra, empty-handed, merely returned the blow. Needless to say, Mohendra was something more than a little angry, and the worthy sepoy reeled with the blow and went down stunned on the road. Upon that, three or four sepoys came up, took hold of Mohendra and, dragging him forcibly to the commander, told the Saheb, "This man has killed one of the sepoys." The Saheb was smoking and a little bewildered with strong drink; he replied, "Catch hold of the rogue and marry him." The soldiers did not understand how they were to marry an armed highwayman, but in the hope that, with the passing of the intoxication, the Saheb would change his mind and the marriage would not be forced on them, three or four sepoys bound Mohendra hand and foot with the halters of the cart bullocks and lifted him into the cart. Mohendra saw that it would be vain to use force against so many, and, even if he could effect his escape by force, what was the use? Mohendra was depressed and sorrowful with grief for his wife and child and had no desire for life. The sepoys bound Mohendra securely to the wheel of the cart. Then with a slow and heavy stride the escort proceeded on its march.

Chapter VIII

POSSESSED of the ascetic's command, Bhavananda, softly crying the name of Hari, went in the direction of the inn where Mohendra had been sitting; for he thought it likely that there he would get a clue to Mohendra's whereabouts.

At that time the present roads made by the English were not in existence. In order to come to Calcutta from the district towns, one had to travel by the marvellous roads laid down by the Mogul emperors. On his way from Padchinha to the town, Mohendra had been travelling from south to north, and it was therefore that he met the soldiers on the way. The direction Bhavananda had to take from the Hill of Palms towards the inn, was also from south to north; necessarily, he too on his way fell in with the sepoys in charge of the treasure. Like Mohendra, he stood aside to let them pass. Now, for one thing, the soldiers naturally believed that the dacoits would be sure to attempt the plunder of this despatch of treasure, and on that apprehension came the arrest of a dacoit in the very highway. When they saw Bhavananda too standing aside in the night-time, they inevitably concluded that here was another dacoit. Accordingly, they seized him on the spot.

Bhavananda smiled softly and said, "Why so, my good fellow?"

"Rogue!" answered a sepoy, "you are a robber."

"You can very well see I am an ascetic wearing the yellow robe. Is this the appearance of a robber?"

"There are plenty of rascally ascetics and Sannyasins who rob," retorted the sepoy, and he began to push and drag Bhavananda. Bhavananda's eyes flashed in the darkness, but he only said very humbly, "Good master, let me know your commands."

The sepoy was pleased at Bhavananda's politeness and said, "Here, rascal, take this load and carry it," and he clapped a bundle on Bhavananda's head. Then another of the sepoys said to the first, "No, he will run away; tie up the rascal on the cart where the other rogue is bound." Bhavananda grew curious to know who was the man they had bound; he threw away the bundle on his head and administered a slap on the cheek to the soldier who had put it there. In consequence, the sepoys bound Bhavananda, lifted him on to the cart and flung him down near Mohendra. Bhavananda at once recognised Mohendra Singha.

The sepoys again marched on, carelessly and with noise, and the creaking of the cartwheels recommenced. Then, softly and in a voice audible only to Mohendra, Bhavananda said, "Mohendra Singha, I know you and am here to give you help. There is no need for you to know just at present who I am. Do very carefully what I tell you. Put the rope that ties your hands on the wheel of the cart."

Mohendra, though astonished, carried out Bhavananda's suggestion without a word. Moving a little towards the cartwheel under cover of darkness, he placed the rope that tied his hands so as to just touch the wheel. The rope was gradually cut through by the friction of the wheel. Then he cut the rope on his feet by the same means. As soon as he was free of his bonds, by Bhavananda's advice he lay inert on the cart. Bhavananda also severed his bonds by the same device. Both lay utterly still and motionless.

The path of the soldiers took them precisely by the road where the Brahmacharin had stood in the highway near the jungle and gazed round him. As soon as they arrived near the hill, they saw under it, on the top of a mound, a man standing. Catching sight of his dark figure silhouetted against the moonlit azure sky, the havildar said, "There is another of the rogues; catch him and bring here: he shall carry a load."

At that a soldier went to catch the man, but, though he saw the fellow coming to lay hold on him, the watcher stood firm; he did not stir. When the soldier laid hands on him, he said nothing. When he was brought as a prisoner to the havildar, even then he said nothing. The havildar ordered a load to be put on his head; a soldier put the load in place, he took it on his head. Then the havildar turned away and started marching with the cart. At this moment a pistol shot rang suddenly out and the havildar, pierced through the head, fell on the road and breathed his last. A soldier shouted, "This rascal has shot the havildar," and seized the luggage-bearer's hand. The bearer had still the pistol in his grasp. He threw the load from him and struck the soldier on the head with the butt of his pistol; the man's head broke and he dropped farther proceedings. Then with a cry of "Hari! Hari! Hari!" two hundred armed men surrounded the soldiery. The men were at that moment awaiting the arrival of their English captain, who, thinking the dacoits were on him, came swiftly up to the cart and gave the order to form a square; for an Englishman's intoxication vanishes at the touch of danger. The sepoys immediately formed into a square facing four ways and at a farther command of their captain lifted their guns in act to fire. At this critical moment someone wrested suddenly the Englishman's sword from his belt and with one blow severed his head from his body. With the rolling of the Englishman's head from his shoulders the unspoken command to fire was silenced for ever. All looked and saw a man standing on the cart, sword in hand, shouting loud the cry of "Hari, Hari" and calling "Kill, kill the soldiers." It was Bhavananda.

The sudden sight of their captain headless and the failure of any officer to give the command for defensive action kept the soldiers for a few moments passive and appalled. The daring assailants took advantage of this opportunity to slay and wound many, reach the carts and take possession of the money chests. The soldiers lost courage, accepted defeat and took to flight.

Then the man who had stood on the mound and afterwards assumed the chief leadership of the attack, came to Bhavananda. After a mutual embrace Bhavananda said, "Brother Jivananda, it was to good purpose that you took the vow of our brotherhood." "Bhavananda," replied Jivananda, "justified be your name." Jivananda was charged with the office of arranging for the removal of the plundered treasure to its proper place and he swiftly departed with his following. Bhavananda alone remained standing on the field of action.

Chapter IX

MOHENDRA had descended from the cart, wrested a weapon from one of the sepoys and made ready to join in the fight. But at this moment it came home clearly to him that these men were robbers and the plunder of the treasure the object of their attack on the soldiery. In obedience to this idea he stood away from the scene of the fight, for to help the robbers meant to be a partner in their ill-doing. Then he flung the sword away and was slowly leaving the place when Bhavananda came and stood near him. Mohendra said to him, "Tell me, who are you?"

Bhavananda replied, "What need have you to know that?"

"I have a need" said Mohendra. "You have done me today a very great service."

"I hardly thought you realized it;" said Bhavananda, "you had a weapon in your hand and yet you stood apart. A landholder are you, and that's a man good at being the death of milk and ghee, but when work has to be done, an ape."

Before Bhavananda had well finished his tirade, Mohendra answered with contempt and disgust, "But this is bad work, — a robbery!"

"Robbery or not," retorted Bhavananda, "we have done you some little service and are willing to do you a little more."

"You have done me some service, I own," said Mohendra, "but what new service can you do me? And at a dacoit's hands I am better unhelped than helped."

"Whether you accept our proffered service or not," said Bhavananda, "depends on your own choice. If you do choose to take it, come with me. I will bring you where you can meet your wife and child."

Mohendra turned and stood still. "What is that?" he cried.

Bhavananda walked on without any reply, and Mohendra had no choice but to walk on with him, wondering in his heart what new kind of robbers were these.

Chapter X

SILENTLY in the moonlit night the two crossed the open country. Mohendra was silent, sorrowful, full of pride, but also a little curious.

Suddenly Bhavananda's whole aspect changed. No longer was he the ascetic, serious of aspect, calm of mood; no longer the skilful fighter, the heroic figure of the man who had beheaded the English captain with the sweep of a sword; no longer had he that aspect with which even now he had proudly rebuked Mohendra. It was as if the sight of that beauty of plain and forest, river and numerous streams, all the moonlit peaceful earth, had stirred his heart with a great gladness; it was as if Ocean were laughing in the moonbeams. Bhavananda became smiling, eloquent, courteous of speech. He grew very eager to talk and made many efforts to open a conversation, but Mohendra would not speak. Then Bhavananda, having no other resource, began to sing to himself.

> "Mother, I bow to thee!
> Rich with thy hurrying streams,
> Bright with thy orchard gleams,
> Cool with thy winds of delight,
> Dark fields waving, Mother of might,
> Mother free!"

The song astonished Mohendra and he could understand nothing of it. Who might be this richly watered, richly fruited Mother, cool with delightful winds and dark with the harvests? "What Mother?" he asked.

Bhavananda without any answer continued his song.

> "Glory of moonlight dreams
> Over thy beaches and lordly streams;
> Clad in thy blossoming trees,
> Mother, giver of ease,
> Laughing low and sweet!
> Mother, I kiss thy feet,
> Speaker sweet and low!

Mother, to thee I bow."

Mohendra said, "That is the country, it is not the Mother."

Bhavananda replied, "We recognize no other Mother. 'Mother and Motherland is more than heaven itself.' We say the motherland is our mother. We have neither mother nor father nor brother nor friend, wife nor son nor house nor home. We have her alone, the richly-watered, richly-fruited, cool with delightful winds, rich with harvests — "

Then Mohendra understood and said, "Sing it again." Bhavananda sang once more.

Mother, I bow to thee!
Rich with thy hurrying streams,
Bright with thy orchard gleams,
Cool with thy winds of delight,
Dark fields waving, Mother of might,
Mother free.

Glory of moonlight dreams
Over thy beaches and lordly streams;
Clad in thy blossoming trees,
Mother, giver of ease,
Laughing low and sweet!
Mother, I kiss thy feet,
Speaker sweet and low!
Mother, to thee I bow.

Who hath said thou art weak in thy lands,
When the swords flash out in seventy million hands
And seventy million voices roar
Thy dreadful name from shore to shore?
With many strengths who art mighty and stored,
To thee I call, Mother and Lord!
Thou who savest, arise and save!
To her I cry who ever her foemen drave
Back from plain and sea

And shook herself free.

Thou art wisdom, thou art law,
Thou our heart, our soul, our breath,
Thou the love divine, the awe
In our hearts that conquers death.
Thine the strength that nerves the arm,
Thine the beauty, thine the charm.
Every image made divine
In our temples is but thine.
Thou art Durga, Lady and Queen,
With her hands that strike and her swords of sheen,
Thou art Lakshmi lotus-throned,
And the Muse a hundred-toned.

Pure and perfect, without peer,
Mother, lend thine ear.
Rich with thy hurrying streams,
Bright with thy orchard gleams,
Dark of hue, O candid-fair
In thy soul, with jewelled hair
And thy glorious smile divine,
Loveliest of all earthly lands,
Showering wealth from well-stored hands!
Mother, mother mine!
Mother sweet, I bow to thee,
Mother great and free!

Mohendra saw the robber as he sang shedding tears. In wonder he asked, "Who are you?"

Bhavananda replied, "We are the Children."

"What is meant by the Children?" asked Mohendra. "Whose children are you?"

Bhavananda replied, "The children of the Mother."

"Good;" said Mohendra, "do the children worship their mother with theft and looting? What kind of filial piety is that?"

"We do not thieve and loot," answered Bhavananda.

"Why, just now you plundered the carts."

"Is that theft and looting? Whose money did we plunder?"

"Why, the ruler's."

"The ruler's! What right has he to the money, that he should take it?"

"It is his royal share of the wealth of the country."

"Who rules and does not protect his kingdom, is he a ruler at all?"

"I see you will be blown one day from the cannon's mouth by the sepoys."

"I have seen your rascal sepoys more than once: I dealt with some today too."

"Oh, that was not a real experience of them; one day you will get it."

"Suppose it is so, a man can only die once."

"But what profit is there in going out of one's way to die?"

"Mohendra Singha," said Bhavananda, "I had a kind of idea that you were a man worth the name, but now I see you are what all the rest of them are, merely the death of ghee and milk. Look you, the snake crawls on the ground and is the lowest of living things, but put your foot on the snake's neck and even he will rise with lifted hood. Can nothing overthrow your patience then? Look at all the countries you know, Magadh, Mithila, Kashi, Kanchi, Delhi, Cashmere, in what other country do men from starvation eat grass? eat thorns? eat the earth white ants have gathered? eat the creepers of the forest? where else are men forced to eat dogs and jackals, yes, even the bodies of the dead? where else can men have no ease of heart because of fear for the money in their chests, the household gods on their sacred seats, the young women in their homes, the unborn children in the women's wombs? Ay, here they rip open the womb and tear out the child. In every country the relation with the ruler is that of protector and protected, but what protection do our Mussulman rulers give us? Our religion is destroyed, our caste defiled, our honour polluted, our family honour shamed and now our very lives are going the same way. Unless we drive out these vice-besodden longbeards, the Hinduism of the Hindu is doomed."

"How will you drive them out?" asked Mohendra.

"By blows."

"You will drive them out single-handed? With one slap, I suppose."

The robber sang:

"Who hath said thou art weak in thy lands,
When the swords flash out in seventy million hands
And seventy million voices roar
Thy dreadful name from shore to shore?"

"But" said Mohendra, "I see you are alone."

"Why, just now you saw two hundred men."

"Are they all Children?"

"They are all Children."

"How many more are there of them?"

"Thousands like these, and by degrees there will be yet more!"

"Even if there were ten or twenty thousand, will you be able with that number to take the throne from the Mussulman?"

"What army had the English at Plassey?"

"Can Englishmen and Bengalis be compared?"

"Why not? What does physical strength matter? Greater physical strength will not make the bullet fly farther."

"Then," asked Mohendra, "why is there such a difference between an Englishman and a Mussulman?"

"Take this first;" said Bhavananda, "an Englishman will not run away even from the certainty of death. A Mussulman runs as soon as he perspires and roams in search of a glass of sherbet. Next take this, that the Englishman has tenacity; if he takes up a thing, he carries it through. "Don't care" is a Mussulman's motto. He is giving his life for a hire, and yet the soldiers don't get their pay. Then the last thing is courage. A cannon ball can fall only in one place, not in ten; so there is no necessity for two hundred men to run from one cannon ball. But one cannon ball will send a Mussulman with his whole clan running, while a whole clan of cannon balls will not put even a solitary Englishman to flight."

"Have you all these virtues?" asked Mohendra.

"No," said Bhavananda, "but virtues don't fall from the nearest tree. You have to practise them."

"Do you practise them?"

"Do you not see we are sannyasins? It is for this practice that we have made renunciation. When our work is done, when our training is complete, we shall again become householders. We also have wives and daughters."

"You have abandoned all those ties, but have you been able to overcome Maya?"

"The Children are not allowed to speak falsely and I will not make a lying boast to you. Who has the strength to conquer Maya? When a man says, 'I have conquered Maya', either he never had any feeling or he is making a vain boast. We have not conquered Maya, we are only keeping our vow. Will you be one of the Children?"

"Until I get news of my wife and daughter, I cannot say anything."

"Come then, you shall see your wife and child."

The two went on their way; and Bhavananda began again to sing Bande Mataram.

Mohendra had a good voice and was a little proficient in singing and fond of it; therefore he joined in the song, and found that as he sang the tears came into his eyes. Then Mohendra said, "If I have not to abandon my wife and daughter, then initiate me into this vow."

"Whoever" answered Bhavananda, "takes this vow, must abandon wife and child. If you take this vow, you cannot be allowed to meet your wife and daughter. Suitable arrangements will be made for their protection, but until the vow is crowned with success, to look upon their faces is forbidden."

"I will not take your vow," answered Mohendra.

Chapter XI

THE day had dawned. That unpeopled forest, so long dark and silent, now grew full of light, blissful with the cooing and calling of the birds. In that delightful dawn, that joyous forest, that "Monastery of Bliss" Satyananda, seated on a deerskin, was performing his morning devotions. Jivananda sat near. It was at such a time that Bhavananda appeared with Mohendra Singha behind. The ascetic without a word continued his devotions and no one ventured to utter a sound. When the devotions were finished, Bhavananda and Jivananda saluted him and with humility seated themselves after taking the dust of his feet. Then Satyananda beckoned to Bhavananda and took him outside. What conversation took place between them, we do not know, but on the return of the two into the temple the ascetic, with compassion and laughter in his countenance, said to Mohendra, "My son, I have been greatly distressed by your misfortune; it was only by the grace of the Friend of the poor and miserable that I was able to rescue your wife and daughter last night." The ascetic then told Mohendra the story of Kalyani's rescue and said at the end, "Come, let me take you where they are."

The ascetic in front, Mohendra behind entered into the inner precincts of the temple. Mohendra beheld a wide and lofty hall. Even in this cheerful dawn, glad with the youth of the morning, when the neighbouring groves glittered in the sunshine as if set and studded with diamonds, in this great room there was almost a gloom as of night. Mohendra could not at first see what was in the room, but by gazing and gazing and still gazing he was able to distinguish a huge image of the four-armed Vishnu, bearing the shell, the discus, the club, the lotus-blossom, adorned with the jewel Coustoobh on his breast; in front the discus called Sudarshan, the Beautiful, seemed visibly to be whirling round. Two huge headless images representing Madhu and Kaitabh were painted before the figure, as if bathed in their own blood. On the left stood Lakshmi with flowing locks garlanded with wreaths of hundred-petalled lotuses, as if distressed with fear. On the right stood Saraswati surrounded by books, musical instruments, the incarnate strains and symphonies of music. On Vishnu's lap sat an image of enchanting beauty, lovelier than Lakshmi and Saraswati, more splendid with opulence and lordship. The Gandharva and Kinnara and God and elf and giant paid her homage. The ascetic asked Mohendra in a voice of deep solemnity and awe, "Can you see all?"

"Yes" replied Mohendra.

"Have you seen what is in the lap of Vishnu?" asked the ascetic.

"Yes," answered Mohendra, "who is she?"

"It is the Mother."

"What mother?"

"She whose children we are," replied the ascetic.

"Who is she?"

"In time you will recognise her. Cry 'Hail to the Mother!' Now come, you shall see."

The ascetic took Mohendra into another room. There he saw an image of Jagaddhatri, Protectress of the world, wonderful, perfect, rich with every ornament. "Who is she?" asked Mohendra.

The Brahmacharin replied, "The Mother as she was."

"What is that?" asked Mohendra.

"She trampled underfoot the elephants of the forest and all wild beasts and in the haunt of the wild beasts she erected her lotus throne. She was covered with every ornament, full of laughter and beauty. She was in hue like the young sun, splendid with all opulence and empire. Bow down to the Mother."

Mohendra saluted reverently the image of the Motherland as the protectress of the world. The Brahmacharin then showed him a dark underground passage and said, "Come by this way." Mohendra with some alarm followed him. In a dark room in the bowels of the earth an insufficient light entered from some unperceived outlet. By that faint light he saw an image of Kali.

The Brahmacharin said, "Look on the Mother as she now is."

Mohendra said in fear, "It is Kali."

"Yes, Kali enveloped in darkness, full of blackness and gloom. She is stripped of all, therefore naked. Today the whole country is a burial ground, therefore is the Mother garlanded with skulls. Her own God she tramples under her feet. Alas, my Mother!"

The tears began to stream from the ascetic's eyes.

"Why," asked Mohendra, "has she in her hands the club and the skull?"

"We are the Children, we have only just given weapons into our Mother's hands. Cry 'Hail to the Mother!'"

Mohendra said "Bande Mataram" and bowed down to Kali.

The ascetic said "Come by this way", and began to ascend another underground passage. Suddenly the rays of the morning sun shone in their eyes and from every side the sweet-voiced family of birds shrilled in song. In a wide temple built in stone of marble they saw a beautifully fashioned image of the Ten-armed Goddess made in gold, laughing and radiant in the light of the early sun. The ascetic saluted the image and said, "This is the Mother as she shall be. Her ten arms are extended towards the ten regions and they bear many a force imaged in her manifold weapons; her enemies are trampled under her feet and the lion on which her foot rests, is busy destroying the foe. Behold her, with the regions for her arms," — as he spoke, Satyananda began to sob, — "with the regions for her arms, wielder of manifold weapons, trampler down of her foes, with the lion-heart for the steed of her riding; on her right Lakshmi as Prosperity, on her left Speech, giver of learning and science, Kartikeya with her as Strength, Ganesh as Success. Come, let us both bow down to the Mother." Both with lifted faces and folded hands began to cry with one voice, "O auspicious with all well-omened things, O thou ever propitious, who effectest all desire, O refuge of men, three-eyed and fair of hue, O Energy of Narayan, salutation to thee."

The two men bowed down with awe and love, and when they rose, Mohendra asked in a broken voice, "When shall I see this image of the Mother?"

"When all the Mother's sons" replied the Brahmacharin, "learn to call the Mother by that name, on that day the Mother will be gracious to us."

Suddenly Mohendra asked, “Where are my wife and daughter?”

“Come” said the ascetic, “you shall see them.”

“I wish to see them once and say farewell.”

“Why should you say farewell?”

“I shall take up this mighty vow.”

“Where will you send them to?”

Mohendra thought for a little and then said, “There is no one in my house and I have no other place. Yet in this time of famine, what other place can I find?”

“Go out of the temple,” said the ascetic, “by the way by which you came here. At the door of the temple you will see your wife and child. Up to this moment Kalyani has eaten nothing. You will find articles of food in the place where they are sitting. When you have made her eat, do whatever you please; at present you will not again meet any of us. If this mind of yours holds, at the proper time I shall show myself to you.”

Then suddenly by some path unknown the ascetic vanished from the place. Mohendra went forth by the way pointed out to him and saw Kalyani with her daughter sitting in the court of meeting.

Satyananda on his side descended by another underground passage into a secret cellar under the earth. There Jivananda and Bhavananda sat counting rupees and arranging them in piles. In that room gold, silver, copper, diamonds, coral, pearls were arrayed in heaps. It was the money looted on the previous night they were arranging. Satyananda, as he entered the room, said, “Jivananda, Mohendra will come to us. If he comes, it will be a great advantage to the Children, for in that case the wealth accumulated in his family from generation to generation will be devoted to the Mother’s service. But so long as he is not body and soul devoted to the Mother, do not take him into the order. As soon as the work you have in hand is completed, follow him at various times and when you see it is the proper season, bring him to the temple of Vishnu. And in season or out of season protect their lives. For even as the punishment of the wicked is the duty of the Children, so is the protection of the good equally their duty.”

Chapter XII

IT was after much tribulation that Mohendra and Kalyani met again. Kalyani flung herself down and wept, Mohendra wept even more than she. The weeping over, there was much ado of wiping the eyes, for as often as the eyes were wiped, the tears began to come again. But when at last the tears had ceased to come, the thought of food occurred to Kalyani. She asked Mohendra to partake of the food which the ascetic's followers had kept with her. In this time of famine there was no chance of ordinary food and vegetables, but whatever there was in the country, was to be had in plenty among the Children. That forest was inaccessible to ordinary men. Wherever there was a tree with fruit upon it, famishing men stripped it of what it bore, but none other than the Children had access to the fruit of the trees in this impenetrable wilderness. For this reason the ascetic's followers had been able to bring for Kalyani plenty of forest fruits and some milk. In the property of the Sannyasin were included a number of cows. At Kalyani's request, Mohendra first took some food, afterwards Kalyani sat apart and ate something of what he had left. She gave some of the milk to her child and kept the rest to feed her with again. Then both of them, overcome with sleep, took rest for a while. When they woke, they began to discuss where they should go next. "We left home" said Kalyani "in fear of danger and misfortune, but I now see there are greater dangers and misfortunes abroad than at home. Come then, let us return to our own house." That also was Mohendra's intention. It was his wish to keep Kalyani at home under the care of some suitable guardian and take upon himself this beautiful, pure and divine vow of service to the Mother. Therefore he gave his consent very readily. The husband and wife, rested from fatigue, took their daughter in their arms and set forth in the direction of Padchinha.

But what way led to Padchinha, they could not at all make out in that thick and difficult forest. They had thought that once they could find the way out of the wood, they would be able to find the road. But now they could not find the way out of the wood itself. After long wandering in the thickets, their circlings began to bring them round to the monastery once more, no way of exit could be found. In front of them they saw an unknown ascetic in the dress of a Vaishnav Gosain, who stood in the path and laughed at them. Mohendra, in some irritation, said to him, "What are you laughing at, Gosain?"

"How did you enter the forest?" asked the Gosain.

"Well, we have entered it, it does not matter how."

"Then, when you have entered, how is it you cannot get out again?" So saying, the ascetic resumed his laughter.

"Since you laugh," said Mohendra, much provoked, "I presume you can yourself get out?"

"Follow me," said the Vaishnav, "I will show you the way. You must undoubtedly have entered the forest in the company of some one of the ascetics. No one else knows the way either into or out of the forest."

On this Mohendra asked, "Are you one of the Children?"

"I am" answered the Vaishnav. "Come with me. It is to show you the way that I am standing here."

"What is your name?" asked Mohendra.

"My name" replied the Vaishnav "is Dhirananda Goswami."

Dhirananda proceeded in front, Mohendra and Kalyani followed. Dhirananda took them out of the forest by a very difficult path and again plunged back among the trees.

On leaving the forest one came after a little to a common with trees. To one side of it there was the highway running along the forest, and in one place a little river flowed out of the woodland with a murmuring sound. Its water was very clear, but dark like a thick cloud. On either bank beautiful dark-green trees of many kinds threw their shadow over the river and in their branches birds of different families sat and gave forth their various notes. Those notes too were sweet and mingled with the sweet cadence of the stream. With a similar harmony the shadow of the trees agreed and mingled with the colour of the stream. Kalyani sat under a tree on the bank and bade her husband sit near. Mohendra sat down, and she took her child from her husband's lap into her own. Kalyani held her husband's hand in hers and for some time sat in silence, then she asked, "Today I see that you are very melancholy. The calamity that was on us, we have escaped; why then are you so sad?"

Mohendra answered with a deep sigh, "I am no longer my own man, and what I am to do, I cannot understand."

"Why?" asked Kalyani.

"Hear what happened to me after I lost you," said Mohendra, and he gave a detailed account of all that had happened to him.

Kalyani said, "I too have suffered greatly and gone through many misadventures. It will be of no advantage to you to hear it. I cannot say how I managed to sleep in such exceeding misadventure, but today in the early hours of the morning I fell asleep, and in my sleep I saw a dream. I saw — I cannot say by what force of previous good works I went there, — but I saw myself in a region of wonder, where there was no solid Earth, but only light, a very soft sweet light as if of a cool lustre broken by clouds. There was no human being there, only luminous forms, no noise, only a sound as if of sweet song and music at a great distance. Myriads of flowers seemed to be ever newly in bloom, for the scent of them was there, jasmines of many kinds and other sweet-smelling blossoms. There in a place high over all, the cynosure of all, one seemed to be sitting, like a dark blue hill that has grown bright as fire and burns softly from within. A great fiery crown was on his head, his arms seemed to be four. Those who sat at either side of him, I could not recognize, but I think they were women in their forms, but so full of beauty, light and fragrance that every time I gazed in that direction, my senses were perplexed, I could not fix my gaze nor see who they were. In front of the Four-Armed another woman's form seemed to be standing. She too was luminous, but surrounded by clouds so that the light could not well manifest itself; it could only be dimly realised that one in the form of a woman wept, one full of heart's distress, one worn and thin, but beautiful exceedingly. It seemed to me that a soft fragrant wind carried me along, pushing me as with waves, till it brought me to the foot of the Four-Armed's throne. It seemed to me that the worn and cloud-besieged woman pointed to me and said, 'This is she, for whose sake Mohendra will not come to my bosom.' Then there was a sound like the sweet clear music of a flute; it seemed that the Four-Armed said to me, 'Leave your husband and come to Me. This is your Mother, your husband will serve her; but if you stay at your husband's side, that service cannot be given. Come away to Me.' I wept and said, 'How shall I come, leaving my husband?' Then the flutelike voice came again, 'I am husband, father, mother, son, daughter; come to Me.' I do not remember what I said. Then I woke." Kalyani spoke and was again silent.

Mohendra also, astonished, amazed, alarmed, kept silence. Overhead the *doyel* began its clamour, the *papia* flooded heaven with its voice, the call of the cuckoo set the regions echoing, the *bhringaraj* made the grove quiver with its sweet cry. At their feet the stream murmured softly between its banks. The wind carried to them the soft fragrance of the woodland flowers. In places bits of sunlight glittered on the waves of the rivulet. Somewhere palm-leaves rustled in the slow wind. Far off a blue range of mountains met the eye. For a long time they remained silent in delight. Then Kalyani again asked, "What are you thinking?"

"I am thinking what I should do. The dream is nothing but a thought of fear, it is born of itself in the mind and of itself it disappears, — a bubble from the waking life. Come, let us go home."

"Go where God bids you," said Kalyani and put her child in her husband's lap.

Mohendra took his daughter in his lap and said, "And you, — where will you go?"

Kalyani, covering her eyes with her hands and pressing her forehead between them, answered, "I too will go where God has bid me."

Mohendra started and said, "Where is that? How will you go?"

Kalyani showed him the small box of poison.

Mohendra said in astonishment, "What, you will take poison?"

"I meant to take it, but — " Kalyani became silent and began to think. Mohendra kept his gaze on her face and every moment seemed to him a year, but when he saw that she did not complete her unfinished words, he asked, "But what? What were you going to say?"

"I meant to take it, but leaving you behind, leaving Sukumari behind, I have no wish to go to Paradise itself. I will not die."

With the words Kalyani set down the box on the earth. Then the two began to talk of the past and future and became absorbed in their talk.

Taking advantage of their absorption the child in her play took up the box of poison. Neither of them observed it.

Sukumari thought, "This is a very fine toy." She held it in her left hand and slapped it well with her right, put it in her right, and slapped it with her left. Then she began pulling at it with both hands. As a result the box opened and the pill fell out.

Sukumari saw the little pill fall on her father's cloth and took it for another toy. She threw the box away and pounced on the pill.

How it was that Sukumari had not put the box into her mouth, it is hard to say, but she made no delay in respect of the pill. "Eat it as soon as you get it;" — Sukumari crammed the pill into her mouth. At that moment her mother's attention was attracted to her.

"What has she eaten? What has she eaten?" cried Kalyani, and she thrust her finger into the child's mouth. Then both saw that the box of poison was lying empty. Then Sukumari, thinking that here was another game, clenched her teeth, — only a few had just come out, — and smiled in her mother's face. By this time the taste of the poison-pill must have begun to feel bitter in the mouth, for a little after she loosened the clench of her teeth of herself and Kalyani took out the pill and threw it away. The child began to cry.

The pill fell on the ground. Kalyani dipped the loose end of her robe in the stream and poured the water into her daughter's mouth. In a tone of pitiful anxiety she asked Mohendra, "Has a little of it gone down her throat?"

It is the worst that comes first to a parent's mind, — the greater the love, the greater the fear. Mohendra had not seen how large the pill was before, but now, after taking the pill into his hand and scrutinising it for some time, he said, "I think she has sucked in a good deal of it."

Necessarily, Kalyani adopted Mohendra's belief. For a long time she too held the pill in her hand and examined it. Meanwhile the child, owing to the little she had swallowed, became a little indisposed; she grew restless, cried, at last grew a little dull and feeble. Then Kalyani said to her husband, "What more? Sukumari has gone the way God called me to go. I too must follow her."

And with the words Kalyani put the pill into her mouth and in a moment had swallowed it.

Mohendra cried out, "What have you done, Kalyani, what have you done?"

Kalyani returned no answer, but taking the dust of her husband's feet on her head, only said, "Lord and Master, words will only multiply words. I take farewell."

But Mohendra cried out again, "Kalyani, what have you done?" and began to weep aloud. Then Kalyani said in a very soft voice, "I have done well. You might otherwise neglect the work given you by Heaven for the sake of so worthless a thing as a woman. See, I was transgressing a divine command, therefore my child has been taken from me. If I disregarded it farther, you too might go."

Mohendra replied with tears, "I could have kept you somewhere and come back, — when our work had been accomplished, I could have again been happy with you. Kalyani, my all! Why have you done this thing? You have cut from me the hand by whose strength I could have held the sword. What am I without you?"

"Where could you have taken me? Where is there any place? Mother, father, friends, all in this terrible time of calamity have perished. In whose house is there any place for us, where is the road we can travel, where will you take me? I am a burden hanging on your neck. I have done well to die. Give me this blessing that when I have gone to that luminous world, I may again see you." With the words Kalyani again took the dust of her husband's feet and placed it on her head. Mohendra made no reply, but once more began to weep. Kalyani again spoke; — her voice was very soft, very sweet, very tender, as she again said, "Consider who has the strength to transgress what God has willed. He has laid his command on me to go; could I stay, if I would? If I had not died of my own will, inevitably someone else would have slain me. I do well to die. Perform with your whole strength the vow you have undertaken, it will create a force of well-doing by which I shall attain heaven and both of us together will enjoy celestial bliss to all eternity."

Meanwhile the little girl threw up the milk she had drunk and recovered, — the small amount of poison that she had swallowed, was not fatal. But at that time Mohendra's mind was not turned in that direction. He put his daughter in Kalyani's lap and closely embracing both of them began to weep incessantly. Then it seemed that in the midst of the forest a soft yet thunder-deep sound arose, —

"O Hari, O Murari, O foe of Kaitabh and Madhu!
O Gopal, O Govinda, O Mukunda, O Shauri!"

By that time the poison had begun to act on Kalyani, her consciousness was being somewhat taken from her; in her half unconscious condition she seemed to herself to hear the words ringing out in the marvellous flutelike voice she had heard in the Vaikuntha of her dream.

"O Hari, O Murari, O foe of Kaitabh and Madhu!
O Gopal, O Govinda, O Mukunda, O Shauri!"

Then Kalyani in her semi-unconsciousness began to sing in a voice sweeter than any Apsara's,

"O Hari, O Murari, O foe of Kaitabh and Madhu!"

She cried to Mohendra, "Say,

"O Hari, O Murari, O foe of Kaitabh and Madhu!"

Deeply moved by the sweet voice that rose from the forest and the sweet voice of Kalyani and in the grief of his heart thinking "God is my only helper," Mohendra called aloud,

"O Hari, O Murari, O foe of Kaitabh and Madhu!"

Then from all sides the sound arose,

"O Hari, O Murari, O foe of Kaitabh and Madhu!"

Then it seemed as if the very birds in the trees were singing,

"O Hari, O Murari, O foe of Kaitabh and Madhu!"

It seemed as if the murmurs of the river repeated,

"O Hari, O Murari, O foe of Kaitabh and Madhu!"

Then Mohendra, forgetting his grief and affliction and full of ecstasy, sang in one voice with Kalyani,

"O Hari, O Murari, O foe of Kaitabh and Madhu!"

From the forest the cry seemed to rise in chorus with their song,

"O Hari, O Murari, O foe of Kaitabh and Madhu!"

Kalyani's voice became fainter and fainter, but still she cried,

"O Hari, O Murari, O foe of Kaitabh and Madhu!"

Then by degrees her voice grew hushed, no sound came from her lips, her eyes closed, her body grew cold, and Mohendra understood that Kalyani had departed to Vaikuntha with the cry of "O Hari, O Murari" on her lips. Then Mohendra began to call out loudly like one frantic, making the forest quiver, startling the birds and beasts.

"O Hari, O Murari, O foe of Kaitabh and Madhu!"

At that time one came and, embracing him closely, began to call with him in a voice as loud as

"O Hari, O Murari, O foe of Kaitabh and Madhu!"

Then in that glory of the Infinite, in that boundless forest, before the body of her who now travelled the eternal way, the two sang the name of Eternal God. The birds and beasts were voiceless, the earth full of a miraculous beauty, — the fitting temple for this highest anthem. Satyananda sat down with Mohendra in his arms.

Chapter XIII

MEANWHILE there was a great commotion in the high road in the capital. The noise went abroad that Sannyasins had plundered the revenue that was being despatched from the royal treasury to Calcutta. Then by order of the Government sepoys and spearmen sped on all sides to seize Sannyasins. Now at that time in that famine-stricken country there was no great number of real Sannyasins; for these ascetics live upon alms, and when people themselves get nothing to eat, there is not likely to be anyone to give alms to the mendicant. Therefore all the genuine ascetics had fled from the pinch of hunger to the country about Benares and Prayag. Only the Children wore the robe of the Sannyasin when they willed, abandoned it when abandonment was needed. Now too, many, seeing trouble abroad, left the dress of the ascetic. For this reason the hungry retainers of power, unable to find a Sannyasin anywhere, could only break the waterjars and cooking-pots of the householders and return with their empty bellies only half-filled. Satyananda alone would at no time leave his saffron robe.

At the moment when on the bank of that dark and murmurous rivulet, on the borders of the high road, at the foot of the tree on the water's verge, Kalyani lay still and Mohendra and Satyananda in each other's embrace were calling on God with streaming eyes, Jamadar Nazir-ud-din and his sepoys arrived at the spot. Forthwith he put his hand on Satyananda's throat and said, "Here is a rascal of a Sannyasin." Immediately another seized Mohendra; for a man who consorts with Sannyasins, must necessarily be a Sannyasin. A third hero was about to arrest the dead body of Kalyani where it lay at length on the grass. Then he saw that it was the corpse of a woman and very possibly might not be a Sannyasin, and did not proceed with the arrest. On the same reasoning they left the little girl alone. Then without colloquy of any kind they bound the two prisoners and marched them off. The corpse of Kalyani and her little daughter remained lying unprotected at the foot of the tree.

Mohendra was at first almost senseless with the oppression of grief and the frenzy of divine love; he could not understand what was toward or what had happened and made no objection to being bound; but when they had gone a few paces, he awoke to the fact that they were being led away in bonds. Immediately it occurred to him that Kalyani's corpse was left lying without funeral rites, that his little daughter was left lying, and that even now wild beasts might devour them, he wrenched his hands apart by sheer force and with the one wrench tore his bonds apart. With one kick he sent the Jamadar sprawling to the ground and fell upon one of the sepoys; but the other three seized him from three sides and once more overpowered and rendered him helpless. Then Mohendra in the wretchedness of his grief said to the Brahmacharin Satyananda, "If only you had helped me a little, I would have slain these five miscreants." "What strength is there" answered Satyananda, "in this aged body of mine, — except Him on whom I was calling, I have no other strength. Do not struggle against the inevitable. We shall not be able to overpower these five men. Come, let us see where they will take us. The Lord will be our protection in all things." Then both of them without farther attempt at escape followed the soldiers. When they had gone a little distance, Satyananda asked the sepoys, "My good fellows, I am in the habit of calling on the name of Hari; is there any objection to my calling on His name?" The Jamadar thought Satyananda to be a simple and inoffensive man, and he said, "Call away, I won't stop you. You are an old Brahmacharin and I think there will be an order for your discharge; this ruffian will be hanged." Then the Brahmacharin began softly to sing,

With the lingering wind in her tresses,
Where the stream its banks caresses,
There is one in the woodland, a woman and fair.
Arise, O thou hero, let speed
Be swift in thy feet to her need;
For the child who is there
Is full of sorrow and weeping and care.

On arriving in the city they were taken to the Chief of Police, who sent word to the Government and put the Brahmacharin and Mohendra for the time into confinement. That was a dreadful prison, for it was seldom that he who entered came out, because there was no one to judge. It was not the British jail with which we are familiar — at that time there was not the British system of justice. Those were the days of no procedure, these are the days of procedure. Compare the two!

Chapter XIV

NIGHT has come. Imprisoned Satyananda told Mohendra 'Today is a day of great rejoicing, because we have been shut up in a prison. Exclaim — 'Haray Muraray.'

Mohendra plaintively repeated — 'Haray Muraray.'

Satya: "Why so distressed, my boy? Had you taken this vow, cutting off all connection with your wife and children would have been a matter of course; you could not then have had any earthly tie to bind you."

Mohendra: "It is one thing to renounce and quite another to suffer the sentence of the God of death. Besides, the power which would have enabled me to take this vow has departed with my wife and daughter."

Satya: "That power shall come. I will give that power. Be initiated in this great *mantra* and do take this great vow."

"My wife and daughter are being devoured by dogs and jackals; the less we talk of a vow the better for all," disgustingly replied Mohendra.

Satya: "Herein set all doubts at rest. The Santans have rightly done the obsequies of your wife and safely housed your daughter."

Mohendra was astonished but did not put much reliance on these words and said, "How do you know it? You have all along been with me"

Satya: "We have been initiated in a great enterprise. The gods show us their bounty. This night you will get the news, and this night you will be liberated from the prison."

Mohendra did not speak anything. Satyananda felt that Mohendra could not see his way to believing him.

Satyananda then said, "You can't believe it? All right, then try." Thus saying Satyananda came up to the door of the prison but what he actually did Mohendra could not see in that darkness; all that he realised was that he was speaking to somebody.

On his return Mohendra asked him, "What shall I try?"

Satya: "At this very moment you will get released from the prison."

No sooner had these words been uttered than the prison doors opened. Somebody got into the cell and inquired "Whose name is Mohendra?'

Mohendra said, "My name."

The newcomer then said, "Your release order has come, you can now go."

Mohendra was first astonished and then thought it was all a hoax. He came out for proof. Nobody resisted his progress. Mohendra proceeded up to the high road. Meanwhile the newcomer told Satyananda, "Maharaj, you too may go; I have come to relieve you."

Satya: "Who are you, is it Dhirananda Gossain?"

Dhira: "Yes Sir."

Satya: "How did you come to be a sentinel?"

Dhira: "Bhavananda has sent me. When I came to the city and learnt that you were in this prison, I fetched here a little *Siddhi* mixed with *Dhutura.* The Khan Saheb who was on duty took it and fell into a deep sleep on this piece of earth as his bed; this uniform and turban and spear which I have worn belongs to him."

Satya: "You get out of this city in this uniform. I shall not do so."

Dhira: "Why, how is that?"

Satya: "To-day is the day of trial for the Santans."

Mohendra returned by this time. Satyananda asked him, "Why do you come back?"

Mohendra: "You are no doubt a god-man, but I shall not leave your company."

Satyananda: "Then stay with me, we shall both be released in another manner."

Dhirananda went out; Satyananda and Mohendra remained inside the prison.

Chapter XV

MANY had heard the Brahmachari's song. Amongst others the sons entered Jivananda's ears. The reader may remember that he was asked to follow Mohendra. He met a woman on the way. She went without food for seven days and lay by the wayside. Jivananda delayed for a few minutes to save her life. After saving the woman, he began to call her ugly names as he now proceeded, the delay being due to her. He saw that his master was being marched by the Mussulmans and the former sang as he went his way. Jivananda knew all the signs of his master — Satyananda. In the gentle breeze by the riverside lives the great woman in the forest. Is there any other woman lying down in starvation by the riverside? So thinking, Jivananda began to proceed by the riverside. Jivananda saw that the Brahmachari himself was being led by the Mussulmans. So to rescue the Brahmachari was his first duty. But Jivananda thought that far other was the meaning of this sign. To do his bidding was greater than to save his life — that was what I first learnt of him. So to do his bidding should be my first effort. Jivananda began to proceed by the riverside. He saw as he went on under the shade of that tree on the riverside the dead body of a woman and a living girl. The reader may remember here, that he did not even see for once Mohendra's wife and daughter and thought they might be Mohendra's wife and daughter, because Mohendra was seen with his master. Be that as it may, the mother was dead and the daughter alive.

"I shall save the girl first, or tiger or bear will eat her up. Bhavananda must be somewhere here; he will see to the proper disposal of the woman's dead body." So thinking, Jivananda took the girl into his arms and went on.

Jivananda entered the deep jungle after taking the girl into his arms. He then crossed the jungle and entered a hamlet. The name of the hamlet is Bhairabipur. Its popular name was Bharuipur. It was inhabited by some common people. There is no other big village near it; and beyond again the jungle. Jungle on all sides a small village nestles within but it is very beautiful. A pasture covered by soft grass. A garden of mango, jack, berry and palm, all wearing soft green leaves; in the middle, a transparent tank full of blue water. Within the water, cranes, ducks and dahuka; on its bank cuckoo and chakrabak; a little away peacocks were cackling aloud. Every house-yard has its cow; within the house its granary, but without its content of paddy in these days of famine. Some roofs have their hanging of bird cage; some walls plain white drawings, and some yards their Vegetable plots. Everything is looking lean, gaunt slender and parched through the effect of famine. Yet the people of this village have retained their grace. The jungles grow varieties of human food and the village people could somehow manage to keep their body and soul together by gleaning food from the forest.

A small house lay within a big mango, grove. There were mud- walls on the four sides as also four sheds on each. The house-holder has cows, goats, one peacock, one Maina and one parrot. He had a monkey which had to be let off as it could not be provided with food. A wooden ricehusker, a granary outside the compound, and flower plants of mallika and jasmine; but they did not blossom this time. Every house-ledge had its spinning wheel but the house itself was somewhat bare of men. Jivananda entered the house with the girl in his arms.

No sooner had Jivananda entered this house than he went to the edge of one of the sheds and started the noise of spinning. The small girl never heard the sound of spinning. Besides, she was crying since she had left her mother and, further frightened by the sound of spinning, she began to cry at the top of her voice. Then a girl of seventeen or eighteen came out of the shed. As soon as she got out she put the finger of her right hand to her right cheek and stood up with a little slant in her neck. "What this, why does brother go on spinning? Where does this girl come from? Brother, have you begotten a daughter, have you married a second time?"

Jivananda put the girl into the lap of this young woman and aimed at her a blow. He then said: — "Wicked girl, you take me to be capable of begetting a daughter — am, I a commonplace house-holder? Have you got milk at home?"

The young woman then said, "Yes, we have milk by all means — will you take it?"

Jivananda said, "Yes, I shall take it."

Then the young woman anxiously went to heat the milk. Meanwhile Jivananda went on plying the wheel with its monotonous noise. The girl ceased crying when ensconced in the lap of the young woman. It is difficult to say what the girl thought; may be, seeing the young woman like a blooming flower, she took her to be her mother. May be the glow of the fire in the oven reached her and therefore she cried out once. On hearing her cry Jivananda said, "Oh Nimi, O burnt-faced, O monkey-visaged, you have not yet been able to heat the milk?"

Nimi replied, "I have finished heating."

With these words she poured the milk into a stone cup and brought it to Jivananda.

Jivananda feigned indignation and said, "I wish I could empty this cup of hot milk over your body. Are you such a fool as to think that it is meant for myself?"

Nimi asked, "For whom is it then meant?"

"Don't you see that it is meant for this baby? Just feed her with this milk."

Nimi then sat down with crossed legs, placed the girl on her lap and set herself to feeding the child with a spoon. All on a sudden a few tears trickled down her cheek. She had given birth to a boy who died, and the spoon belonged to that child. Nimi at once wiped off the tears with her hand and asked Jivananda as she smiled. "My brother, whose daughter is this, brother?"

Jivananda said, "That is no concern of yours, you burnt-faced!" Nimi said, "Will you make a gift of this girl to me?"

Jivananda said, "What will you do with it, supposing I give it to you?"

Nimi: "I shall feed her on milk, dandle her and bring her up." Once more the tears came into Nimi's eyes, once more Nimi wiped them with her hands, once more she laughed.

Jivananda said: What will you do with her? You will have many children yourself.

Nimi: That may be so. Give me this girl now, afterwards, you can take her away.

Jivananda: Then take her and go to your death. I shall come now and then and see her. The child is a Kayastha's girl. Now I am going.

Nimi: How can that be *dada?* It is late. You must eat a little and go or I swear you eat my head.

Jivananda: Eat your head and at the same time eat a little food — I cannot do justice to two things at the same time. Leave your head alone and bring me some rice.

Nimi then started serving the rice still carrying the girl on one arm.

Nimi placed a wooden seat and scattered a little water on the floor and wiped it. Then she served Jivananda with rice which was white, soft and flaky like the petals of jessamine flowers, a dish of wild figs cooked into a curry, carp fish stewed in spices and milk. When sitting to eat, Jivananda said, "Nimi! Sister! Who says there is a famine? Has the famine not reached your village?"

Nimi said: Why should the famine not reach here? A terrible famine is raging here. But we are only two people. Whatever there is in the house, from this store, we give to others and eat ourselves. There was rain in our village, don't you remember? You told me at that time that it rains in the forest. In our village some paddy could be cultivated. Every one else went to the city and sold the rice. We did not sell our rice.

Jivananda: Where is my brother-in-law?

Nimi hung her head and said, "He has gone out with two or three seers of rice. Some one, I believe, asked for it."

For long Jivananda had not had such a good meal. Without wasting further words he started eating noisily and finished the rice and other food within a short time.

Now Nimaimoni had cooked only for herself and her husband. She had given her own share of food to Jivananda, but seeing the stone platter empty she was a little taken aback and now brought her husband's share of food and served it on Jivananda's platter. Without noticing anything amiss, Jivananda filled the big cavity called his stomach with the food. Then Nimaimoni asked, "Dada, will you eat anything more?"

Jivananda said: "What else is there?"

Nimaimoni replied: "There is a ripe jack fruit."

Nimi brought that ripe jack fruit and gave it to Jivananda. Without making any excuses Jivananda Goswami sent that ripe jack fruit into the same cavity. Then Nimai said laughingly — "Dada, there is nothing else."

Her Dada said "Then, let me go, I shall come another day and have my food with you."

There being no alternative Nimai gave Jivananda water to wash his hands. Whilst giving the water, Nimai said. "Dada, will you keep one request of mine?"

Jivananda: What?

Nimai: Keep it or I swear you eat my head.

Jivananda: Tell me what it is, you burntface.

Nimai: Will you keep the request?

Jivananda: What is it? Tell me first.

Nimai: I swear you eat my head. Oh! I fall at your feet.

Jivananda: All right. I swear. I eat your head, yes! you may fall at my feet. Now tell me what it is.

Nimai then pressed her two hands joined together tightly with fingers interlocked and looked at them. Once she looked at Jivananda, then looked down at the ground and at last said,

"Shall I call your wife once?"

Jivananda raised the jug of water with which he was washing his hands and made as if to throw it at Nimai. He then said, "Return my girl tome. I shall come another day and return your rice and lentils. You monkey! you burnt-face! That which should never be said — you say that to me!

Nimai said: "Let that be! I admit I am a monkey, I am a burnt-face — shall I call your wife?"

Jivananda: I am going.

Saying this Jivananda tried to leave the house with rapid strides.

Nimai went and stood at the door way. She bolted the door and stood with her back against it. — "Kill me first and then go. Without seeing your wife you will not be able to go."

Jivananda said: "Do you know how many men I have killed?" This time Nimai said in real anger. "You have indeed done great things. You will abandon your wife, you will kill people — and I shall fear you! I am the child of the same father as yourself. If killing people is something to boast about kill me and boast about it."

Jivananda laughed and said: "Go and call her. Call any sinning woman you wish to. But if again you say such a thing to me, I may or may not say anything to you but I shall set that rascal on a donkey with his face turned towards its tail, shave his head, pour whey on it and turn him out of his village."

In her heart of hearts she said. "I too shall then be relieved." Saying this to herself she laughingly left the room. She entered a thatched hut near by. In the hut was seated a woman with unkempt hair, dressed in a cloth tom and knotted in a hundred places spinning. Nimai went and said, "Sister, quick!" The woman asked, "What is the hurry about? Has your husband beaten you that I have to apply oil on the wound?"

Nimai: You have hit the nail nearly on the head. Have you any oil?

The woman brought the vessel of oil and gave it to Nimai. Nimai took handfuls of oil and started oiling the hair of that woman. Soon she had bound her hair into a passable knot. Then giving her a cuff she said. "Where is that sari of Dacca muslin which you had?" The woman, a little surprised said, "What! Have you gone mad?"

Nimai slapped her on the back and said, "Bring put that cloth." To see the fun the woman brought out the *sari.* To see the fun — for even with such sorrow in her heart the spirit of fun and play had not been wiped out from it. In youthful freshness, like a full blown lotus was the beauty of her full womanhood. With unkempt hair, without food, without proper clothes, still that shining beauty beyond imagination flamed forth even through that cloth torn and knotted in a hundred places. In her complexion what shimmer of light and shade, in her eyes what glamour, on her lips what a smile, in her heart what patience! She had no proper food, yet what grace and beauty in that body! She was not dressed in proper clothes and ornaments yet her beauty was completely expressed through what clothes she wore, as is the lightening through the clouds, as is genius in the mind, as is song in sound, as is happiness in death — so in that beauty there was a charm quite indescribable.

The woman smiled (none saw that smile) as she took out that *sari* of Dacca muslin. She said, "Well Nimi, what will you do with it?" Nimai said, "You will wear it." She asked, "What will happen if I wear it?" Then Nimai encircled her soft arms round that graceful neck and said. "Dada has come. He has asked you to go and see him." The woman said. "If he has asked me to go, why this *sari* of Dacca muslin? Let me go as I am now." Nimai slapped her face, but she took Nimai by the shoulders and forced her out of the hut. She said, "Come, let me wear this rag and go and see him." She would not change her *sari* through any persuasion. There being no alternative Nimai had to agree. Nimai took her and went with her to the door of her own house. She pushed her into the room, closed the door and chained it from outside and herself stood in front of the door.

Chapter XVI

THE woman who entered was almost twenty-five but she did not appear older than Nimai. She entered the room clothed in a dirty cloth tom and knotted together, but it seemed that with her beauty the whole room was lighted. It seemed as if some plant in which the buds were covered with thick foliage had suddenly burst into bloom. It seemed that somewhere a vessel of rose water tightly closed had been broken open and its fragrance dispersed. It seemed that somebody had cast scented incense into dying embers which flamed and became luminous with sweet odour. The lovely woman who had entered the room began searching for her husband rather hesitatingly. At first she could not find him. Then she found Jivananda in the courtyard, his head resting against the trunk of a mango tree, weeping. The beautiful woman approached him slowly and took his hand. It cannot be said that there were no tears in her eyes. God knows that the unshed sea of tears held back in her eyes if allowed to flow would have been enough to flood Jivananda. But she did not allow it to flow. She held Jivananda's hand in her own and said, "Do not weep. I know your tears are flowing for me. Do not weep for me. As you have chosen to keep me I am happy so to live."

Jivananda raising his bent head dried his eyes and said to his wife. "Santi, why do you wear this dirty cloth tom and knotted in a hundred places. You are not in need of food and raiment?"

Santi replied — "Your wealth is stored for you. I do not know what to do with money. When you return, when you once more take me back —"

Jivananda exclaimed, "Take you back — Santi! Have I abandoned you?"

Santi — "No, you have not abandoned me. I mean when your vow is completed, when you are able once more to love me — "

Before Santi could finish her words Jivananda locking Santi in a tight embrace resting his head on her shoulders remained silent for a long time. At last sighing he exclaimed — "Why did I see you?"

Santi —"Why did you see me? You have broken your vow!"

Jivananda — "Let it be broken, I can always do penance for that. I am not anxious on that account. But having seen you I cannot return. For this I told Nimai that I should not see you — that seeing you I could not return. On one side religion, wealth, desire, liberation, the entire world — and again my vow, the sacrificial fire, religious practices, all these and on the other — you. I cannot at all times realise if these were balanced which scale would be the weightier. My country is after all peaceful — what shall I do with it? If I could but get a fraction of an acre of land, with you I could build a heaven on it. What use is the country to me? As to the sorrows of my countrymen — one who has abandoned a wife like you, no man can be more sorrowful than him? One who has seen you clothed in tom clothes knotted in a hundred places, who can be poorer than him? You are my helpmate in my religion. He who has abandoned such a support, what to him is the true religion? For what religion do I wander from place to place, from forest to forest my gun on my shoulder killing people? Why should I thus burden myself with sins? I do not know if the Santans will ever possess the world. But you are my possession. You are greater than the world to me, you are my heaven. Come home with me. I shall return no more."

For a while Santi could give no reply. And then she said, "Fie! You are a hero. My greatest happiness in the world is that I am the wife of a hero. For a worthless woman will you abandon the path of the hero? Do not love me. I do not want that happiness. But do not ever forsake your faith — the path of the hero. Only tell me one thing before you leave, what penance must you perform for breaking your vow."

Jivananda replied. "Penance? Gifts in charity, fast, a fine of twelve kahan of cowries."

Santi smiled a little and said. "I know what the penance is. Is it the same penance for one as for a hundred failings?"

Jivananda asked in sadness and surprise — "Why these words?"

Santi. — "I have one favour to ask. Before meeting me again do not perform any penance."

Jivananda then replied laughingly, "You may rest assured about that. Without seeing you once more I shall not die. There is no hurry about dying. I shall not stay here any more. But I have not yet feasted my eyes enough on your beauty. One day undoubtedly I shall see you till my heart is full. One day surely our desires will be fulfilled. I am now leaving. Keep one request of mine, abandon these clothes and go and live in my paternal home."

Santi asked, "Where will you go now?" Jivananda — "I shall now go to our *math* in search of the Brahmachari. The manner in which he went into the city has caused me some anxiety. If I do not find him in the temple, I must go to the city."

Chapter XVII

BHAVANANDA was sitting in the *math* chanting the sacred name of Hari. At this time Jnanananda one of the *Santans* came to him with a sad face. Bhavananda asked, “Gossain, why this heavy countenance?”

Janananda replied, “Danger is threatening for yesterday’s incident, as soon as the Mussulmans see any saffron robed person he is arrested. All the *Santans* have discarded their saffron robes. Our chief Satyananda alone in saffron robes has gone towards the city all alone. Who knows, the Mohammedans might arrest him”

Bhavananda answered. — “The Mohammedan is still unborn in Bengal who can keep him in prison. I know Dhirananda has already followed him. Still I also shall go to the city once. Please take charge of the *math*”

Thus saying, Bhavananda entered a secret chamber and from a large chest took out some clothes. Suddenly Bhavananda was transformed. In place of saffron coloured robes he wore *churidar pyjamas*, *merzai* and *kaba,* on his head an *amama,* the Mohammedan turban, on his feet *nagra.* From his face he had wiped off the sacred Tripundra marks of sandal paste. In raven black beard and mustaches his fine face looked wonderfully handsome. Seeing him at the time one would mistake him for a young Moghul. Thus dressed and having armed himself Bhavananda left the *math.* Two miles further there were two hillocks, covered with dense trees. Between the two hills there was a lonely place where a number of horses were kept. This was the stable of the *math.* Bhavananda from amongst these untied a horse and mounting it rode on towards the city.

As he rode, suddenly he stopped. On the wayside near the roaring river bank, like a star which had dropped from the skies, like a streak of lightening which had descended from the clouds, he saw a dazzlingly beautiful woman’s form lying. There was no sign of life in her. Beside her lay an empty phial of poison: Bhavananda was surprised, keenly sorrowful, afraid. Like Jivananda, Bhavananda too had not seen Mohendra’s wife and daughter. The reasons which made Jivananda suspect them to be the wife and daughter of Mohendra, were unknown to Bhavananda. He had not seen the Brahmachari and Mohendra being arrested, the child too was no longer there. Seeing the empty phial he surmised that some woman had taken poison and died. Bhavananda sat beside the corpse. For a long time with his head resting on his hands he mused. He then examined the body touching the head, the armpit, the hands, the side, with expert knowledge. Then he said to himself, "There is time yet, but why save her?" For long he considered the matter. Then he entered the forest, and took some leaves from a tree. He rubbed the leaves in his hand and taking the juice he forced it between the lips and clenched teeth of the corpse. Later he forced some juice up the nostrils. He rubbed the body with the juice. He went on repeating the same process, now and then placing his hand near the nostrils to see if there was any respiration. It seemed that all his care would be fruitless. But after, much anxious examination, Bhavananda's face bore some marks of hopefulness. He seemed to feel a faint trace of respiration on his fingers. He then applied more juice of that leaf, till the respiration became more pronounced. Feeling the pulse he saw that the heart had started working. At last gradually, like the first rosy flush of dawn in the east, like the first opening of the lotus bloom, like the first quiver of love, Kalyani began to open her eyes. Seeing which Bhavananda raised that semiconscious form on his horse and rode fast towards the city.

Chapter XVIII

BEFORE evening the Society of the Santans all knew that Satyananda Brahmacharin and Mohendra had both been captured and imprisoned in the city. Then in ones, twos, tens and hundreds Santans began to assemble and fill the forest surrounding the temple. All were armed, an angry fire glowed in their eyes, there was pride in their faces and on their lips a vow. At first a hundred, then a thousand, then two thousand, thus more and more men began to assemble. Then standing at the entrance of the math, his sword in his hand, Jnanananda spoke in a loud voice — "We have long contemplated breaking this nest of pernicious birds (Babui) totally destroying this Mussulman city and throwing it into the river. We must burn this nest with fire and once more purify the earth. Brethren, that day has dawned. The *Guru* of our *Guru,* our highest *Guru*, he who is all knowledge, who is forever pure in action, and is the well-wisher of the country and who for once more preaching the religion of the *Santans* has vowed to sacrifice his body, whom, we regard as the *Avatar* of Vishnu, wlio is the means of our freedom, today he is a prisoner in the prison of the Mussulmans. Is there no edge to our swords?" Then stretching his arms Jnanananda asked, "Is there no strength in our arms." Again striking his breast he said, 4s there no courage in this heart? Brethren repeat with me —

> O Hari, O Murari, O enemy of
> Madhu and Kaitava!

"He who has destroyed Madhu and Kaitava, he who has destroyed Haranyakashipu, Kangsa, Dantabakra, Sishupa! — he who has killed all these unconquerable Asuras, and hearing the terrible grinding noise of whose *chakra* the deathless Sambhu himself was afraid — he who is unconquerable and the giver of victory in battle, we are his devotees, with his strength our arms are gifted with endless strength. He is will incarnate. If he wills it we shall be victors in battle. Come, let us go and reduce to dust that city of the Mussulmans. Let us purify with fire that den and cast it into the river. Let us break that nest of pernicious birds and scatter its twigs and straws to the four winds. Oh my brothers, repeat after me —

O Hari, O Murari, O enemy of
Madhu and Kaitava!"

Then from the forest arose a terrible cry. From a hundred thousand voices at once re-sounded —

"O Hari, O Murari, O enemy of
Madhu and Kaitava!"

A thousand swords clashed at once, a thousand tall spear-heads were at once raised on high. A thousand hands clapped. A thousand shields granted on the backs of the soldiers. The animals of the forest were frightened by the terrible din and fled. The disturbed birds rose shrieking to the sky and covered it with their wings. At that time a thousand war drums were sounded at once and shouting — "O Hari, O Murari, O enemy of Madhu and Kaitava!" the Santans in ordered rank marched out of the forest. Then with slow measured steps loudly crying the name of Hari in that dark night they advanced towards the city. And there was heard, as they went, the rustling of dead leaves, the rattling of arms, the half suppressed chant with loud cries of "Hari Bol" in between. Slowly, gravely, with angry ferocity, that army of Santans came to the city and struck fear in the hearts of the citizens. At this sudden thunder-stroke the citizens fled none knows where. The guardians of the city with their guards remained actionless.

The Santans first went to the public prison and broke it open. They killed the guards and freeing Satyananda and Mohendra they lifted them high and danced in joy. A loud cry of Hari-bol resounded in the air. After freeing Satyananda and Mohendra, wherever they found the home of a Mussaiman they burnt it. Then Satyananda said. "Let us return — no need of this useless destruction."

Meanwhile having heard of the ravages of the Santans, the authorities sent a regiment of Sepoys to suppress them. They not only had guns but also a canon. The Santans hearing of their coming left the forest of Ananda and advanced to fight with them. But lathis and spears or even twenty or twenty-five guns are useless before a canon. The Santans were defeated and started to fly.

PART II

Chapter I

AT a very early age in her childhood Santi lost her mother. Of the influences which built up Santi's character this was the chief. Her father was a Brahmin teacher. In his home there were no other women.

Thus it happened, when Santi's father used to teach in his Tol, Santi used to sit beside him. Some of the students resided in the Tol. At other times Santi would sit beside them and play. She would climb on their laps or shoulders. They too would pet her.

The first result of spending her childhood amongst men, was that Santi did not learn to dress as a girl or if she did, she left off dressing thus. She wore her cloth like a boy and if any one dressed her as a girl she took off her cloth and tucked it up like boys. The students of the Tol did not their hair in a girlish knot at the back of their head. Santi too did not tie her hair thus — and for sooth, who was to do it for her? With a wooden comb the students of the Tol combed her hair which fell in locks and ringlets on her back and shoulders, on her arms and cheek. The students used to adorn their faces with sacred marks and besmear themselves with sandal wood paste. Santi too would do likewise. As she was not allowed to wear the sacred thread like them she would cry bitterly. But at the time of offering morning and evening devotions she would sit with them and imitate their every action. In the absence of their teacher the pupils would with a few obscene Sanskrit quotation make up one or two indecent stories. These Santi learnt like a parrot. Like a parrot she did not know their meaning.

The second result was, that, as soon as Santi began to grow up, whatever the students learnt Santi too began to learn. She knew not a word of grammar, but she learnt by heart with their commentaries the slokas (verses) of Bhatti, Raghu, Kumar, Naishad. Seeing this Santi's father saying to himself, "Let the inevitable happen," started heron Mugdhabodh (grammar). Santi learnt very quickly. Her father was surprised. With the grammar he taught her some books of literature. After that all was lost in confusion. Santi's father died.

Then Santi became homeless. The Tol wound up. The students left.

But they loved Santi. They could not desert her. One of them in pity took her to his home. It is he who afterwards entered the society of Santans as Jivananda. We shall therefore call him Jivananda.

At that time Jivananda's parents were alive. Jivananda properly introduced the girl to them. His parents asked "Who is to take the responsibility of another's daughter?" Jivananda replied, "I have brought her. I shall bear her responsibility." Jivananda's parents said, "It is well." Jivananda was unmarried, Santi was of marriageable age. So Jivananda married her.

After the marriage everyone started regretting the step. They all understood that the action had not been wise. Santi would not dress like a girl. She would not tie her hair like a girl, she would not remain indoors. She would join the young boys of the locality and play with them. Near Jivananda's house there was a forest. Santi would enter the forest alone and search for peacocks, deer and strange flowers and fruits. Her father and mother-in-law at first told her not to go, then scolded her, then beat her and at last kept her locked in a room. These hindrances annoyed Santi very much. One day finding the door open, without telling any one Santi left the house and went away.

Going to the forest, she picked flowers and dyed her clothes in saffron and dressed herself as a young Sannyasin. At that time throughout Bengal there were bands of wandering Sannyasins. Santi begged her bread from door to door and reached the road to the sacred city of Jagannath. Soon on that road appeared a band of Sannyasins. Santi joined this band.

The Sannyasins of those times were not like the present day Sannyasins. They were organised, learned, strong, trained in the art of warfare, and possessors of other good qualities and accomplishments. In a way they were rebels who used to rob the King of his revenue. When they saw strong well-built young boys they kidnapped them. They trained them and initiated them as one of their band. Thus they were called kidnappers.

Santi as a young Sannyasin entered one of these bands. At first seeing her delicate body they were not willing to take her. But when they saw her keeness, her cleverness and ability in work they very willingly took her as one of themselves. Santi remaining with them learnt gymnastics and was trained in the use of all weapons of war, thus becoming hardy. With them she traversed many lands, saw many fights and learnt the art of war.

Soon the unmistakable signs of her budding womanhood become apparent. Many of the Sannyasins came to know that this disguised boy was really a girl. But the Sannyasins were mostly true celibates. No body referred to the fact.

Amongst the Sannyasins there were many scholars. When they saw that Santi had a fair knowledge of Sanskrit a scholarly Sannyasin started teaching her. I have already said that most of the Sannyasins were true celibates, but not all. This scholar certainly was not. Or seeing Santi's young budding beauty he was charmed and distressed by sensual urges. He started to teach her literature full of obscene details, and read to her commentaries of the same nature. This did not harm Santi. Rather it benifitted her. Santi was not acquainted with maiden modesty. Now she became subject to modesty natural to womanhood. To crown her manly firmness the clear lustre of the radiance of womanhood came and still further enhanced her virtues. Santi gave up her studies.

As a hunter pursues a deer, wherever Santi's teacher saw Santi he began to pursue her. But through her gymnastic training she had acquired strength which even a man could envy. As soon as her teacher approached her she would greet him with sounding blows and these blows were by no means of a mean order. One day finding Santi in a lonely place the Sannyasin caught told of Santi's hand in such a strong grip that Santi could not release it with her best efforts. But unluckily for the Sannyasin this was Santi's left hand. With her right hand Santi struck such a fierce blow on the Sannyasin's forehead that he fell fainting to the ground. Santi left the band of Sannyasins and fled.

Santi was fearless. Alone she started in search of her homeland. Because of her courage and the strength of her arms she was able to proceed without much hindrance. Begging her bread or sustaining herself on wild fruits and gaining victory in many a fight Santi reached the home of her father-in-law. She found that her father-in-law had died. But her mother-in-law did not receive her into the house for fear of being outcasted. Santi left her home.

Jivananda was at home. He followed Santi and stopping her on the way asked her, "Why did you leave my house? Where have you been so long?" Santi told the truth. Jivananda knew how to distinguish between truth and falsehood. He believed Santi.

The charmed arrow which is said to have been framed from the light of the glamourous glance full of the sweet desire of the *Apsaras* is not usually wasted by Cupid on a pair already united in wed-lock. Even on full moon night the British light the streets with gas; Bengalis pour oil on a head already well-oiled, and even apart from such unnecessary actions of human beings, in nature, we see that sometimes the moon remains shining in the sky even after sunrise: the God Indra sends rain even over the ocean. In the chest which is already filled to overflowing, the God of wealth carries his riches, the God of Death carries away the remaining one from the man whose home he has already emptied. Only the God of love is more wise. Where the marriage tie has already united a pair, he does not waste his labour. Leaving the whole responsibility to Prajapati, the presiding deity over births, he goes in search of those whose crimson heart's blood he can drink. But perhaps today Cupid was without any occupation. Suddenly he wasted two of his flowery arrows. One struck Jivananda's heart, and the other striking the heart of Santi made her for the first time realise that it was a woman's heart — a thing of extreme tenderness. Like a bud wetted by the first drops of rain freed from the early clouds, Santi suddenly flowered into womanhood and with delighted eyes gazed at Jivananda. Jivananda said, "I will not forsake you, as long as I do not return stand here."

Santi replied — "Will you really come back?"

Jivananda without replying, without looking on either side, in the shade of that grove of coconut trees by the way side kissed Santi and thinking he had drunk nectar left the spot.

Having explained things to his mother, Jivananda took leave of his mother and returned. His sister Nimai had recently been married to a resident of Bhairabipur. Between Jivananda and his brother-in- law a bond of affection had grown. Jivananda went to Bhairabipur taking Santi with him.

His brother-in-law gave Jivananda some land. Jivananda built a cottage on it. Jivananda lived there happily with Santi. Living constantly in the company of her husband the masculine hardness of Santi s character gradually disappeared or remained out of sight. The grace of womanhood flowered anew day by day in Santi. Like a joyous dream their lives were passed. But suddenly that joyous dream was Jivananda under the influence of Satyananda accepting the of the Santan religion left Santi and went away. Their first meeting after Jivananda had left Santi was effected by the trick of Nimai. It is this which has been described in the preceding chapter.

Chapter II

AFTER Jivananda had left her. Santi went and sat on the raised platform outside Nimai's hut. Nimai with the child in her arms came and sat near Santi. Santi was no longer weeping. She had wiped her tears, put on a cheerful countenance and was smiling slightly. She was a little serious, a little thoughtful, a little absent minded. Nimai understanding her thoughts said, "At least you have seen him."

Santi did not reply. She remained silent. Nimai saw that Santi would not tell her thoughts. She did not like to confide her thoughts to anyone. Nimai turned the conversation to other topics. She said — "My sister-in-law, see what a nice child."

Santi asked — "Where did you find the child? When did you get a child?"

Nimai replied — "You will be the death of me. Go to Yama's (Death's) abode. This is Dada's child."

Nimai did not say these words to tease Santi. When she said 'dada's child," she meant the child whom she got from dada. Santi did not understand this. She thought Nimai was trying to tease her. So she said, "I did not ask about the father of the child but about the mother." Nimai having received a due retort, felt somewhat small and replied, "I do not know whose child it is, sister. Dada picked it up from somewhere. I did not find time to enquire. These are days of famine. Many people are leaving their children on the way side. How many people have come to us even to sell their children. But who will take the responsibility of another's child?" Once more tears came to Nimai's eyes. Nimai wiped her tears and said, "Seeing the child was so beautiful, so plump, fair as the moon, I begged the child as a gift from Dada."

After that for a long time Santi talked to Nimai about various things. At last when Nimai's husband returned home Santi got up and went to her own hut. Entering her hut she shut the doors and took out some ashes from the fire place and laid it aside. The cooked rice which she had cooked for herself she threw on the remaining embers. After that she stood immersed in deep thought for a long time. She then said to herself, "What I have so long determined, I shall do today. The hope for which I did not do so all these days is now fulfilled. Fulfilled or unfulfilled I do not know. My existence seems pointless. That which I determined to do, I shall do. The penance which is demanded for breaking the vow once is the same as that which is demanded for breaking the vow a hundred times."

Thus thinking to herself Santi, threw the cooked rice into the fire and brought some fruit from the forest. Instead of rice she ate the fruit. Then she took out the *sari* of Dacca muslin which Nimaimoni had tried to force her to wear and tore its border. What remained of the cloth she coloured in saffron. By the time she had dyed and dried the cloth it was evening. When it was evening Santi with the doors shut occupied herself in a surprising manner. She cut off a portion of her long uncombed hair and kept it aside. What remained she twisted into matted locks. Her unkempt hair was transformed into wonderfully thick mass of matted locks. Then she tore half of the saffron cloth and wrapped it about her beautiful body. It formed the nether garment. With the other half she covered her bosom. In the room there was a tiny mirror. After a long time Santi now took it out. Having taken it out she gazed at her own reflection in the mirror. Then she said, "Ah! How shall I manage it?" Then casting aside the mirror, she took the cut hair and made it into a beard and mustaches but could not wear them. She thought to herself — "Fie! How can that be? In the old days I could do this unashamed but now it is no longer possible. But in order to get round the old man I had better keep them." Thinking thus Santi tied the hair in her cloth. Then bringing out a large deer-skin from within, she tied it in a knot about her neck and thus covered herself from her neck to her knee. So dressed, that young Sannyasin slowly surveyed the whole room. At the 2nd watch of night, Santi dressed as a Sannyasin, opened the door and alone entered the depths of the forest. The nymphs of that forest in the dead of night heard this marvellous song echoing through the forest —

Clatter! Clatter! Where ridest thou
    With flying feet?
To the wars I go, hinder not
    Oh my sweet!
Hari! Hari! Hari! Hari!
'Tis my battle cry,
    In the waves of War shall I plunge
Death defy,

Whose art thou? None be thine?
    Why follow me?
So away to the wars, no woman can
    Enchantment be.

Lord of heart! Leave me not,
    I entreat;
War music sounds; hark my dear!
    War drums do beat!

My impatient horse desireth war,
    Hear him neigh;
Swift flies my heart, no more at home
    Can I stay.
So away to the wars! No woman can
    Enchantment be!

Chapter III

THE next day in a secret chamber of Anandamath the three leaders of the San tans with broken hopes were sitting talking. Jivananda asked Satyananda — "Maharaj, why are Gods so displeased with us. For what fault of ours have we been defeated by the Mussulmans?"

Satyananda replied. "The Gods are not displeased with us. In war there is both victory and defeat. The other day we were victorious. Today we have been defeated. He who wins last is the true victor. I am quite certain that He who has so long been kind to us, the wielder of the club, and the chakra, the holder of the conch shell and the lotus, the mighty Banamali will once more be kind to us. The great vow which we have taken touching his feet, certainly we must perform that vow. If we fail we shall suffer eternal punishment in hell. I have no doubt about our ultimate good fortune. But just as without the grace of the Gods no success can be attained, in the same way human effort is also required. The reason of our defeat is that we are without proper arms. To face shot and shell, to face the gun and cannon, lathis and spears are useless. Thus for want of proper effort on our part we were defeated. Our duty now is that we should not be in want of these weapons.

Jivananda: That is a most difficult task.

Satyananda: A difficult task, Jivananda? Being a Santan how can you say such a thing? For Santans there is no work which is too difficult to be performed.

Jivananda: How shall we gather these arms? Command us.

Satyananda: For gathering them I shall go on pilgrimage to night. Till I return, do not undertake any great enterprise. But keep up the unity of the Santans, provide food and clothes for them and collect ample funds for the Mother's victory, keep our treasury filled. This is the duty which I lay upon you two.

Bhavananda said: How will you collect arms by going on a pilgrimage? It is difficult to buy cartridges, shells, guns and cannons and send them from one place to another. Besides where will you find them in such quantities, who will sell them, and who will bring them?

Satyananda: We cannot accomplish our purpose by buying them. I shall send artisans who must prepare them here.

Jivananda: How is that? Here in Ananda Math?

Satyananda: That is not possible. For a long time I have been thinking out some means of accomplishing this. God has today given me the means. You were telling me, God is not favourable to us. But I see that God is in our favour.

Bhavananda: Where will the factory be established.

Satyananda: At Padachinha

Jivananda: How is that? How can it be established there?

Satyananda: Otherwise why have I been so keen about making Mohendra take the vow?

Bhavananda: Has Mohendra taken the vow?

Satyananda: He has not taken the vow, but he will do so. To-night I shall initiate him.

Jivananda: We have not seen you trying hard to make Mohendra take the vow. What is the condition of his wife and girl child and where have they been kept? To-day I found a little girl child by the river side and went and kept her with my sister. Near her a beautiful woman lay dead. Were they Mohendra's wife and girl child? It appeared to me as if they were?

Satyananda: They were his wife and daughter.

Bhavananda startled in surprise. He understood now that the woman whom he had revived through his medicine was Mohendra's wife Kalyani, but at this time he did not think it necessary to reveal anything about the matter.

Jivananda asked: "How did Mohendra's wife die?

Satyananda: By taking poison.

Jivananda: Why did she take poison?

Satyananda: God ordered her in dream to kill herself.

Bhavananda: Was that command given in order to accomplish the work of the Santans?

Satyananda: I heard so from Mohendra. Now it is evening, I shall go for my evening prayers. After that I shall initiate the new Santans.

Bhavananda: Santans? Why, besides Mohendra does anyone else have the audacity to be your own disciple.

Satyananda: Yes, one more new person. I have never seen him before. Today for the first time he has come to me. He is a mere youth. I have been extremely pleased with his words and his ways. He appeared to be pure gold. I entrust the duty of training him to Jivananda, because Jivananda is an adept in winning people's hearts. I am going. There is one advice that remains to be given to you. Listen to it with great attention.

Then both with folded hands said. "Command us."

Satyananda said: "If either of you have erred or if you err before I return, do not do penance for it before my return. After my return penance will be essential."

Thus saying Satyananda went to his own quarter. Jivananda and Bhavananda looked at each other. Bhavananda said, "Was the advice meant for you?"

Jivananda: "Probably, I went to my sister's house to keep Mohendra's daughter there."

Bhavananda: "That is not a fault. That is not forbidden. Did you see your wife?"

Jivananda said: "Perhaps, Gurudev thinks so."

Chapter IV

AFTER finishing his evening prayers Satyananda called Mohendra and said: "Your daughter is alive."

Mohendra: Where, Maharaj?

Satyananda: Why do you say Maharaj to me?

Mohendra: Because everyone says so. The head of a math is addressed as Rajah. Where is my daughter, Maharaj?

Satyananda: Before you hear that, tell me one thing for certain. Will you accept the religion of the Santans?

Mohendra: There is no doubt about that. I am determined.

Satyananda: Then do not want to know where your daughter is.

Mohendra: Why, Maharaj?

Satyananda: He who accepts this vow cannot keep in touch with his wife, son, daughter or any other relation. If he sees the face of his wife or children he must perform penance. As long as the goal of the Santans is not attained you cannot see your daughter's face. So if you have decided to accept the vow of the Santans then it is useless to know the whereabouts of your child, you will not be able to see her.

Mohendra: Why this difficult rule, my lord?

Satyananda: The work of a Santan is most difficult. He who sacrifices everything alone deserves to accomplish this work. He whose heart is bound in the chains of *maya,* like a kite attached to a peg, he cannot leave the earth and soar to heaven.

Mohendra: Maharaj, I have not been able to understand properly what you are saying. He who sees the face of his wife and children, can he not deserve to do great work?

Satyananda: If we see the faces of our wives and children, we forget the work of the Gods. The rule of the Santan Dharma is this, that, whenever it is necessary a Santan must sacrifice his life. When you remember your daughter's face can you leave her and die?

Mohendra: Even if I do not see her can I forget her?

Satyananda: If you cannot forget her, do not take this vow.

Mohendra: Have all the Santans forgotten their wives and children and taken this vow? Then the number of the Santans must be very few.

Satyananda: Santans are of two kinds. Those who are initiated and those who are uninitiated. Those who are uninitiated are either householders or beggars. They only come at the times of war. They take their share of plunder or other reward and go away. Those who are initiated sacrifice their all. They are the guides of the association. I do not request you to be our uninitiated Santan. At the time of war there are many wielders of lathies and lances. Unless you are initiated you cannot do any responsible work of the association.

Mohendra: What is the initiation? Why should I be initiated? I have already been, initiated by my *Guru* and taken a *mantra.*

Satyananda: You will have to discard that *mantra.* You will have once more to take a *mantra* from me.

Mohendra: How shall I discard my *mantra*?

Satyananda: I shall instruct you in that method.

Mohendra: Why should I have to take a new *mantra*?

Satyananda: The Santans are Vaishnavas.

Mohendra: I do not understand this. Why are the Santans Vaishnavas? To the Vaishnavas non-violence is the highest religion.

Satyananda: That is the Vaishnavism of Chaitanya Dev. The Vaishnavism which was the outcome of the atheistic Buddhist religion—non-violence is its sign. The sign of true Vaishnavism is the suppression of the wicked and the salvation of the world. Because Vishnu is the preserver of the world. Ten times he has taken form in order to save the world. In order to destroy Daityas such as Keshi, Hiranya Kasipu, Madhu Kaitava, Mura, Naraka etc., Rakshashas like Ravana or in order to destroy in battle kings like Sishupala, He has taken birth. It is He who is the Conqueror, the Giver of victory, the Saviour of the world and the deity of worship of the Santans. The Vaishnava religion preached by Chaitanya Deva is not the real Vaishnava religion, it is only half a religion. The Vishnu of Chaitanya Deva is Love incarnate. But God is not only Love incarnate, He is also infinite Power. The Vishnu of Chaitanya Deva is all Love. The Vishnu of the Santans is all Power. We are Vaishnavas of both ideal. But we are both half Vaishnavas. Can you follow me?

Mohendra: No. All these are novel ideas to me. In Kasimbazar I met a Christian priest. He spoke in the same way i.e. "God is Love. You should love Jesus." You speak in the same way.

Satyananda: I am explaining our doctrines to you as all our ancestors have done. Have you heard that the three *gunas* reside in God?

Mohendra: Yes, Sattwa, Raja, Tama — these three gunas.

Satyananda: Well! Each of these *gunas* has a separate mode of worship. From Sattwa comes compassion and its allied virtues. You must attain it through *bhakti* or devotion. The followers or Chaitanya do this. From Raja His *Sakti* is born. This is attained through war — through the suppression or the enemies of the Devas. We do this. And through Tama, God has assumed willingly the four-armed and other forms. Through the gift of garlands, sandal-wood paste etc. we should worship that *guna.* The average man does that. Do you now understand?

Mohendra: I have understood. The Santans then are a particular sect of devotees.

Satyananda: Yes, that is so. We do not want kingly power. Only because the Mussulmans are the enemies of God we want to destroy them totally.

Chapter V

AFTER Satyananda had finished conversing with Mohendra, he entered the inner chamber of the temple which was adorned with that huge four-armed image of great loveliness. What beauty reigned there! Innumerable tapers, carved out of gold and precious stones lit the room. Heaps of flowers decoratcd the room pleasing the senses with their fragrance. In the temple some one else was seated softly chanting "Harey Murarey." As soon as Satyananda entered the room he arose and did obeisance to Satyananda touching his feet. Brahmachari asked him, "Will you be initiated?"

The other replied. 'Take compassion on me and initiate me."

Then Satyananda addressing him and Mohendra said, "Have you both bathed, fasted and purified yourselves by self-control?"

Both replied. "Yes."

Satyananda: Will you both swear before God that you will observe the rules of the Santans?

Both: "We agree."

Satyananda: As long as the salvation of the Mother is not attained will you eschew the life of a householder?

Both: "We agree"

Satyananda: Will you leave your parents?

Both: "We will leave them."

Satyananda: Your brothers and sisters?

Both: "We will renounce them."

Satyananda: Relations and servants?

Both: "We will renounce all."

Satyananda: Riches and enjoyments?

Both: "We hereby renounce everything."

Satyananda: Will you conquer all sensual enjoyments? Will you never sit on the same seat with a woman?

Both: We shall not sit on the same seat with a woman. We shall conquer all sensual enjoyments.

Satyananda: Swear before God that either for yourself or for your people you will not earn money. That which you will earn you will give to the Vaishnava treasury.

Both: We shall do so.

Satyananda: For the true religion will you take up arms and fight?

Both: We shall do so.

Satyananda: You will never fly or turn back in war?

Both: No.

Satyananda: If you break your oath?

Both: We shall mount a lighted pyre or take poison and thus embrace death.

Satyananda: One more thing. What about your caste? What caste are you? Mohendra is a Kayastha. What is the caste of the other?

The other person replied. "I am a young Brahmin."

Satyananda: It is very well. Will you consent to give up your caste? All Santans belong to the same caste. In this great vow we do not distinguish between Brahmins and Sudras. What is your opinion?

Both: We shall not make any distinction. We are all the children of the same Mother.

Satyananda: Then I shall initiate you. Do not break the vows you have just taken. Murari himself is the witness. He who is the destroyer of Ravana, Kangsha, Hiranyakashipu, Jarasandha, Sishupal etc., He who is the Knower of all our hearts, He who is the all-Conqueror, He who is the all-Powerful, the Ruler of the universe who dwells equally in the thunder of Indra or the claws of a cat, He it is who will destroy the breaker of vows and send him to eternal damnation.

Both: "Be it so."

Satyananda: Sing *Bande Mataram*.

Both in that quiet temple sang this song of praise to the Mother Then the Brahmachari with proper rites initiated them.

Chapter VI

AFTER the initiation Satyananda took Mohendra to a lonely place. Both sat down. Satyananda said, "My child, since you have taken this great vow, we have concluded that God is in our favour. Through you a great work of the Mother will be accomplished. Carefully listen to my instructions. I do not ask you to partake in guerilla warfare in forests. Return to *Padachinha.* In your own home you will have to stay and observe the vows of a Sannyasin.

Hearing this Mohendra was both surprised and depressed. He did not reply. The Brahmachari continued — "We have now no dwelling place where if a strong band of soldiers comes, we can with sufficient food shut ourselves up for even ten days without danger. We have no fort. You have a large house, your village is under your own control. I wish to build a fortress there. If we surround *Padachinha* with a moat and at intervals build outposts for soldiers and on the embankment place cannons, a very good fort can be built. Go and live in your home. By and by two thousand Santans will go there. The fort and the embattlements must be built by them. You will also construct there a good iron vault. That will be the treasury of the Santans. Chests filled with gold will be sent one by one by me. With that money you will do this work. And I shall bring from all places skilled craftsmen. When these artisans come, you will establish a factory at *Padachinha*, There you will manufacture cannons, shells, gunpowder and guns. That is why I am asking you to go to your home."

Mohendra agreed.

Chapter VII

MOHENDRA having done obeisance at the feet of Satyananda left. The second disciple who had been initiated that same day came and did obeisance at the feet of Satyananda. Satyananda having blessed him permitted him to sit on the black deer-skin. After some pleasant conversation he asked him, "Well, you have deep faith in Krishna, have you not?"

The disciple said, "How can I say so? That which I think to be faith may be hypocrisy or self-deception."

Satyananda pleased with him replied, "You have thought well. You should perform such duties whereby your devotion can daily grow deeper. I bless you that your efforts may bear fruit; you are very young of age. My son, by what name shall I call you? I have not yet asked you that."

The new disciple replied. "Call me by what name soever pleases you. I am a slave of Vaishnavas."

Satyananda: Because of your youth we wish to call you Navinananda. So you can adopt this name. But there is one thing I wish to ask you. What was your name previously. Even if there be a bar to telling me your name, still you should speak out. If you tell me your name it will not be revealing it to others. The essence of the Santan dharma is this, that, that which is not to be spoken out, that too must be told to the *guru.* There is no harm in telling it to me.

The disciple: My name is Santiram Deva Sharma.

Satyananda: "Your name is Santimani the sinner."

Thus saying Satyananda twisting in his left hand his disciple's: long raven black beard gave it a pull. The false beard came off and Satyananda said, "Fie my daughter, you wish to deceive even me and if you must deceive me, why at this age this long beard? But even if you had shortened your beard, your voice, the glances of your eyes, can you hide them? If I were so foolish could I accomplish so much?"

Santi, poor soul had already covered her eyes with both hands and was sitting with bent head. Immediately afterwards lowering her hands from her face and fixing her enchanting eyes on the old man's face she said, "My lord, what fault have I committed? Is there never strength to be found in the arms of a woman?"

Satyananda: As water may be held in the small hollow made by the hoof of a cow.

Santi: Do you ever test the strength of the Santans?

Satyananda: I do so.

Thus saying Satyananda brought a steel bow and some wire and said — "You will have to string this steel bow with this wire." The bow string must be a yard in length. Whilst stringing the bow the bow often unbends itself and throws down the person stringing it. He who can string this bow is indeed a strong man."

Santi took the bow and arrow and examining it minutely asked: "Have all the Santans passed this test?"

Satyananda: No, by this test I have only been able to examine their strength.

Santi: Has any one been able to pass this test?

Satyananda: Yes, only four men.

Santi: May I ask who they are?

Satyananda: There is no bar to your knowing it. One of them is myself.

Santi: The others?

Satyananda: Jivananda, Bhavananda, Jnanananda.

Santi took the bow and without difficulty stringing it threw it at the feet of Satyananda.

Satyananda was surprised, afraid and astounded. After a little while he asked. "Are you a goddess or a mere woman?"

Santi with folded hands replied, "I am only a woman but I am a Brahmacharini."

Satyananda: How is that? Are you a child widow? No! child widows cannot have this strength. They live on one meal a day only.

Santi: I am a married woman.

Satyananda: Your husband has disappeared?

Santi: No! His whereabouts is known. I have come in search of him.

Suddenly like the sun shining through the clouds, memory lit up the mind of Satyananda.

Satyananda said. Jivananda's wife's name was Santi. Are you Jivananda's wife?

Now Santi covered her face with her matted locks. It seemed that the tusks of several elephants had fallen over and veiled the sun.

Satyananda continued, "Why have you come to commit this sin?"

Immediately Santi threw back her matted locks and with uplifted face and replied, "What sinful behaviour, my lord? If a wife follows the path of her husband is it sinful behaviour? If in the Santan-dharma this is regarded as sinful behaviour then the Santan-dharma is a base religion. I am his partner in religion. He is practicing his vows. I too have come to practice these vows with him."

Having heard the fiery speech of Santi and seeing her uplifted head, her shoulders thrown back, her trembling lips, her bright yet tearful eyes, Satyananda was well pleased. He said, "You are a chaste wife indeed. But my daughter a wife is only a partner in the duties of a house-holder. What place can she have in his heroic deeds?"

Santi: What great hero has been a hero without a wife? If Rama had not Sita, would he have been a hero? How many wives had Arjuna? Can you count them? Bhima's strength was as great as his wives were numerous. How many examples must I cite and why should I have to cite examples to you?

Satyananda: That is true. But what hero goes to the battle field with his wife?

Santi: When Arjuna was fighting with the army of the Jadavas from the air, who was driving his chariot? If Draupadi had not been with them would the Pandavas have fought in the battle of Kurukshetra?

Satyananda: That may be so. But they were demi-Gods. The mind of ordinary men are attracted by women so that they are distracted from their purpose. Because of this the vow of the Santans is this, that, they will not be seated on the same seat as a woman. Jivananda is my right arm. Do you want to break my right arm?

Santi: I have come to strengthen your right arm. I am a Brahmacharini and I shall remain a Brahmacharini. I have come only to practise my religion, not to see my husband. I am not overwhelmed with sorrow at the separation from my husband. Why should I not be a partner in the religion my husband has embraced? I have come for this purpose.

Satyananda: It is well. I shall test you for some days.

Santi asked: "Shall I be able to remain in Anandamath?"

Satyananda: Where can you go today?

Santi: After that?

Satyananda: Like the goddess Bhawani your brow flames like fire. Why should you burn the Santans?

Saying this and blessing Santi he asked her to depart.

Santi said to herself, "Just wait old chap. Does my brow flame like fire? Am I a burnt brow (an unlucky woman) or is your mother a burnt brow?"

Really Satyananda had not meant this. He had referred to the lightening of her glances. But can an old man say this to a young woman?

Chapter VIII

SANTI had gained permission that night to remain in the Math. Many rooms were empty. A servant called Gobardhan — he too was a Santan of a low order — took a taper and showed Santi the rooms. Santi did not like any of them. Losing all hopes, Gobardhan was taking Santi back to Satyananda. Santi said: "Brother Santan, there are several rooms on this side — we have not seen them."

Gobardhan replied: "These are very good rooms indeed, but there are people in them already."

Santi: Who occupy them?

Gobardhan: The big generals occupy them.

Santi: Who are the big generals?

Gobardhan: Bhavananda, Jivananda, Dhirananda, Jnanananda. Ananda Math is full of Ananda.

Santi: Let us see their rooms.

Gobardhan first took Santi to Dhirananda's room. Dhirananda was reading the chapter on Drona from the Mahabharata — how Abhimanyu fought with the seven heroes on their chariots. His mind was immersed in this. He did not speak. Santi left the room without saying anything.

After this Santi entered Bhavananda's room. Bhavananda with eyes uplifted was meditating on a certain face. Whose face I do not know, but it was a very beautiful face. Raven black sweet scented curling hair fell upon a pair of beautifully arched pencilled eye brows, and in the midst was a crescent shaped forehead of extreme loveliness where the dark shadow of death was cast. As if there death and immortal beauty, were engaged in a struggle. Her eyes were closed, her brow peaceful, her lips blue, her cheeks pale, her nose cold, her bosom uplifted, the breeze was blowing on her clothes and disarranging them. Then as the moon hidden amidst autumn clouds gradually lights the clouds and appears in her full glory, as the morning sun, reflecting its golden rays on the white fleecy cloud is itself lit and lights the whole sky, bringing joy over land and water, to insects and all creatures, thus gradually the beauty of life was animating that corpse. Ah! What beauty! Bhavananda was meditating on it. He did not speak. His heart yearned for the beauty of Kalyani. He did not cast a glance at the beauty of Santi.

Santi then went to another room. She asked. "Whose room is this?"

Gobardhan replied: "This room belongs to Jivananda Thakur."

Santi: Who is he? Why is no one here?

Gobardhan: He has gone somewhere. He will return immediately.

Santi: This is the best room.

Gobardhan: Still, you cannot occupy this room.

Santi: Why?

Gobardhan: Jivananda Thakur stays in this room.

Santi: He can find another room for himself if he wishes.

Gobardhan: That is not possible. He who occupies this room he may be called the head of the Math. Everything is done here according to his wishes.

Santi: Alright, you may go. If I cannot find a room I shall stay under a tree.

Saying this and having dismissed Gobardhan Santi entered that room. Having entered it she took the black deer-skin which belonged to Jivananda, spread it on the floor, brightened the taper, and taking one of Jivananda's books began to read it.

After some time Jivananda returned. Although Santi was dressed as a man he immediately recognised her and said, "What is this, Santi?'

Santi slowly laid by the book and looking at Jivananda's face said, "Who is Santi, Sir?"

Jivananda was amazed. At last he said, "Who is Santi, Sir? Why, are you not Santi?"

Santi replied with contempt, "I am Navinananda Goswami." Saying this once more she turned her attention to the book she was reading.

Jivananda laughed loudly. He said, "This is a new farce indeed. Well Navinananda, why are you here?"

Santi replied: "Amongst gentlemen it is the custom, when one is newly acquainted, to address each other in terms of respect and address them as 'Sir' etc. I too am not speaking disrespectfully to you. Then why are you addressing me familiarly?"

"As you please, Sir," Saying this Jivananda put his cloth about his neck and with folded hands said, "Most humbly your servant now requests to tell him why you have come from Bharuipur to this humble home."

Santi very seriously replied, "I do not see any necessity for mockery either. I do not know Bharuipur, I have come this day to embrace the religion of the Santans and I have been initiated."

Jivananda: What terrible misfortune! Is it true?

Santi: Why misfortune? You too are initiated?

Jivananda: You are a woman.

Santi: How is that? How did you come to that conclusion?

Jivananda: I thought my wife was a woman.

Santi: Have you a wife?

Jivananda: At least that is what I knew.

Santi: It is your belief that I am your wife?

Jivananda again with folded hands and his doth about his neck very humbly replied, "Certainly, Sir."

Santi: If such an amusing idea has occurred to you, then what is your duty, can you tell me that?

Jivananda: I should forcibly take off your upper garment and kiss you.

Santi: This is your evil thought or your too great devotion towards *ganjika*. When you were initiated you swore, you would not sit on the same seat with a woman. If you believe me to be a woman — this kind of mistaking a rope for a snake often occurs — then you should sit on a different seat. It is against your duty too to talk to me.

Thus saying Santi once more put her attention to her book. Being defeated Jivananda made a separate bed for himself and lay down.

PART III

Chapter I

BY the grace of God the ill-omened Bengalee year 1276 ended Having sent to the land of Yama six annas (three-eighth) of the people of Bengal — who knows how many crores — that cursed year itself was swallowed up in the gaping jaws of Time. In the year 1277 God was gracious. There was good rain. The earth became green with copious crops, those who had survived ate their fill. Many people were ill due to complete or semi-starvation. They could not bear the increased food. They died of this. The earth was full of vegetation but without men. In all the villages uninhabited houses became the dwelling place of animals and became the cause of the fear of ghosts. In many villages hundreds of fertile fields remained uncultivated and unfertile, or were filled with jungle. The country became full of jungles. Where the laughing green cornfields were to be seen, where numberless cows and buffaloes grazed, those gardens which were the pleasure resorts of the young men and women of the village, these gradually became dense forests. One, two, then three years passed. The jungles increased. Those places where human beings had lived happily now tigers hungry for human flesh came and pursued deer and other animals. In those places where bands of beautiful young women used to go with their companions joking and laughing making sweet music with the anklets which decked their painted crimson feet, bears now made their holes and nursed their young. In those places where children in their tender age in the evening like freshly bloomed jessamines used to laugh the frank laugh which satisfies the heart out of sheer exuberance, there today in bands the intoxicated elephants used to tear the trunks of the trees. Where the festival of Durga Puja would take place, the foxes made holes. On the platform constructed for Dol ceremony owls took refuge. In the theatre arena poisonous snakes even in the Jay time looked for frogs. In Bengal crops grew but there were no people to consume them. Market produce grew, but there was none to purchase them. The peasant ploughed the fields but did not get money in return and could not pay the rent of the landlord. The state confiscated the land of the landowner who thus having lost their all began to get poorer. The earth became fertile, still men did not become rich. None had money in their homes. People robbed and ate. Thieves and robbers became rampant. Good men in fear hid themselves in their houses.

On the other hand the Santans each day with the leaves of the Tulsi plant and with sandalwood-paste began to worship the feet of Vishnu. If any one possessed guns or pistols they would snatch them away. Bhavananda had said, "Brothers, if there is a choice between a room-full of diamonds, corals and precious stones and a broken gun, leave the diamonds, corals and precious stones and bring the broken gun."

After that they sent spies to the villages. The spy went to the villages and to every Hindu they saw they said, "Brothers, will you worship Vishnu?" Thus gathering bands of twenty or twenty-five they came to the villages of the Mussulmans and burnt their houses. When the Mussulmans were busy in saving their lives the Santans used to plunder their all and distribute the plunder among the new initiates of Vishnu, then they would bring the villagers who were pleased with the plunder to the temple of Vishnu and initiate them as Santans. People saw that it was profitable to become Santan. Specially people were disgusted at the bad government and anarchy which prevailed under Muslim rule. Because of the disappearance of Hinduism, many Hindus were eager to establish Hinduism. As the days went by people in hundreds and thousands came and did obeisance at the feet of Jivananda and Bhavananda and in bands went on all sides to punish the Mussulmans. Wherever they got hold of government officials they would beat them or even kill them. Wherever they could get state money they would plunder the money and bring it home. Wherever they came across the villages of the Mussulman's they would set fire to them and reduce them to ashes. The local officials in order to punish the Santans began to send large numbers of soldiers. But now the Santans were well organised, armed and proudly militant. The Mussulman soldiers could not advance against their powerful array. Where they did try to advance the Santans fell on them with great force and would scatter them entirely to the loud cries of "Haribol." If at any time the Mussulman soldiers did overcome a band of Santans. immediately another band would fall on them, none knows from where, and cut off the heads of the Mussulmans and go away crying out, "Hari! Hari!" At this time Warren Hastings, the rising sun of the British community in India, was the Governor-General. At his residence at Calcutta he made an iron chain and thought to himself. "With this chain I shall bind India with her islands and her seas." Some day God on his throne undoubtedly had said — "Be it so," but that day was still distant. Today the terrible echoing cries of Hari shook even Warren Hastings.

At first Hastings tried to suppress the rebellion by soldiers of Fouzdar. But their soldiers were so demoralised that if they ever heard the name of Hari being uttered even by an old woman they would fly. So losing all hopes Hastings sent an astute soldier named Captain Thomas at the head of a regiment of the East India Company to quell the rebellion.

Captain Thomas having reached the place began to excellent arrangements for suppressing the rebellion. He mingled with the well armed and well trained really strong soldiers both British and Indian of the East India Company, soldiers belonging to Mussulman state and to the zamindars. Then taking these mixed companies of soldiers he divided them into suitable bands and appointed deserving commanders over them. Then he divided the country side among them and told each commander that he should, like a fisherman, cast his nets and drag the country clean. "Wherever you see rebels like ants you must crush them." The soldiers of the Company taking either rum or *ganja* as it pleased them, fixing bayonets to their guns went to kill the Santans. But the Santans were now innumerable and unconquerable. The soldiers of Captain Thomas were cut like corn by the scythes of the peasants. His ears were deafened with the cries of Hari! Hari!

Chapter II

AT that time the East India Company owned many silk factories. At Shivagram there was a factory of this kind. Mr. Dannyworth was the factor or head of that factory. During those days there were good arrangements for the protection of these factories. Thus it was that Mr. Dannyworth could somehow save his life. But he had been forced to send his wife and daughters to Calcutta and himself had suffered from the depredations of the Santans. Captain Thomas with some three or four bands of soldiers had come and was staying in that district. Now seeing the enthusiasm of the Santans some ruffians belonging to some of the lowest castes such as Hari, Dome, Bagdi, Buno were encouraged to rob others. They attacked the food convoy of Captain Thomas. Seeing the cart-loads of good flour, clarified butter, rice and fowls which were going for the troops of Captain Thomas, they could not control their greed. They attacked the carts but a few blows from the butt ends of the guns in the hands of Captain Thomas's soldiers made them return. At once Captain Thomas sent the report, "To-day with 157 soldiers 14730 rebels had been defeated. Of the rebels 2153 had died, 1223 wounded and seven were taken prisoners." Only the last item was true. Captain Thomas thinking himself the victor of a second battle of Blenheim of Rossbach twirling his mustaches and stroking his beard fearlessly went from place to place and advised Mr. Dannyworth, that, as the rebellion had been quelled, he could bring his wife and children from Calcutta. Mr. Dannyworth said, "I shall do so, only stay here ten days and let the place be a little quieter." In the house of Mr. Dannyworth there were good fowls and sheep reared for food. There was too plenty of good cheese. Many wild game birds were served at his table. His bearded cook was a second Draupadi in cooking. Thus it was that without any objections Captain Thomas went on living at his home.

On the other hand Bhavananda was fretting with impatience. He was thinking as to when he could cut the head of this Captain Thomas and gain the title of a second Sambarari. At that time the Santans did not realise that the British had come for the salvation of India. How could they understand this? Even the Englishmen who were the contemporaries of Captain Thomas did not know this. This thought was only in the mind of God. Bhavananda was thinking — One day I shall destroy this brood of Asuras. Let them gather together. Let them be a little careless, let us now remain at a little distance. So they kept at some distance. Captain Thomas untroubled by the Santans who were like thorns at his side was able to put his full attention to the virtues of Mr. Dannyworth's excellent cook.

The Captain was very fond of hunting. Sometimes in the forest near Shivagram he would go to hunt. One day along with Mr. Dannyworth riding on horseback, and taking with him some hunters Captain Thomas went out for hunting. To tell the truth, Captain Thomas was extremely courageous. In strength and prowess even among Englishmen he was unequalled. The depth of that forest teemed with tigers, bears and wild buffaloes. After advancing some distance the hunters refused to go further. They said, "There is no road to go further, we cannot go." Mr. Dannyworth also had once escaped from such a terrible tiger in that forest that he too was unwilling to go. All of them wished to return. Captain Thomas replied. "You may go back. I shall not." Thus saying the Captain entered the depths of the forest.

Really in that forest there was no pathway. His horse could not enter. But Captain Thomas, leaving his horse behind with his gun on his shoulder alone entered the forest. Having entered the forest he searched on all sides for tigers but could see none. What he saw was that at the foot of a great tree surrounded by flowering creepers some one was seated. A young Sannyasin with his beauty seemed to light the forest. It seemed that the flowers in full bloom touching that heavenly body had increased in sweet odour. Captain Thomas was astonished. Immediately afterwards he became very angry. Captain Thomas knew the language of the country well. He asked. "Who are you?"

The Sannyasin replied: "I am a Sannyasin."

The Captain asked: "You are a rebel?"

Sannyasin: "What is that?"

Captain: "I shall shoot you."

Sannyasin: "Shoot away."

The Captain was hesitating if he should shoot or not. Immediately at lightening speed the young Sannyasin fell upon him and snatched the gun from his hand. He then threw off the deerskin hiding his bosom. He pulled off his matted locks. Captain Thomas saw a wonderfully beautiful woman. Laughingly the woman said; "Sahib, I am a woman. I do not hurt any one. I only ask you one question — the Hindus and Mussulmans are fighting, why do you intervene? Return home."

Captain Thomas: Who are you?

Santi: You see I am a Sannyasini. I am the wife of one of those with whom you have come to fight.

Captain Thomas: Will you stay in my house?

Santi: How? As your mistress?

Captain Thomas: You can stay as my wife but there will be no marriage.

Santi: I too have a request to make. In our house there was tame monkey. Recently the monkey has died. The cage is empty. I shall put a chain about your waist. Will you stay in that cage? There are very good bananas in our garden.

Captain Thomas: You are a very spirited woman, I am pleased with your courage. Come to my home. Your husband will die in the fight. Then what will happen to you?

Santi: Then let both of us make an agreement. The fight will take place in three or four days. If you win I shall remain as your mistress. I agree to that in case you are still alive. And if we win, you will come to our cage and dress up as a monkey and eat bananas, will you not?

Captain Thomas: Bananas taste very nice. Have you some now?

Santi: Take your gun. It is not possible to talk to such a barbarian.

Santi threw down the gun and went away laughing.

Chapter III

SANTI left Captain Thomas and fleet-footed as a deer entered into the forest. After a while Captain Thomas heard a woman's voice singing

> "This wave of youth who can tide?
> O Hari, O Murari! O Hari, O Murari!"

Then somewhere to the sweet sound of a Sarang the song was played —

> "This wave of youth who can tide?
> O Hari, O Murari! O Hari, O Murari!"

Then with it there mingled a man's voice —

"This wave of youth who can tide?

O Hari, O Murari! O Hari, O Murari!"

The three voices mingled together in song and the creepers of the forest vibrated with it. Santi went on singing —

> "This wave of youth who can tide?
> O Hari, O Murari! O Hari, O Murari!"
> In the waters strong breeze
> My new boat, it floats with ease;
> See the boatman the helm doth seize—
> O Hari, O Murari! O Hari, O Murari!"
> The barrier of sand is broken brother!
> Our dear hopes who can smother?
> The rising tide is in the river,
> Who can stem or stop it ever?
> O Hari, O Murari! O Hari, O Murari!

And once more on the Sarang was played —

> "The rising tide is in the river,

Who can stem or stop it ever?"
O Hari, O Murari! O Hari, O Murari!

Where the forest had so deepened that it was impossible to see from outside what was within, Santi entered the forest. There hidden among the branches and leaves there was a small hut made of logs, thatched with leaves, with a plank flooring which was cemented with mud paste. Santi entered the hut lifting the creepers which covered the doorway. In the hut Jivananda was sitting and playing on the Sarang.

Seeing Santi Jivananda asked, "After so long is the rising tide in the river?"

Santi asked, "Can the river-tide flow in the waters of canals and pools?"

Jivananda said sadly, "Well Santi, for breaking my vow once my life is already forfeit. Whatever is a sin must be atoned for. I would have atoned for it by now too but for your request. But a severe fight can no longer be delayed. In that battlefield I must perform that penance. This life must be sacrificed. The day of my death — "

Santi without allowing him to proceed said. "I am your wife, tied in holy wedlock to you; I am your religious partner, your support in religion. You have embraced an extremely difficult religion. In order to help you in practicing it I have left our home and am living in the forest so that the two of us together may practice our religion. I shall help you in your religion. Being your partner in it why should I hinder you? Marriage is for this life as well as for the life to come. The marriage that is for this life, think that it has not taken place. Our marriage is for the life to come. In the life to come it will be twice as fruitful. But why talk of penance? You have committed no sin. Your vow is that you will not be seated on the same seat with a woman. Why, you have never done so. Why then talk of penance? Alas! My lord, you are my guru, shall I teach you your religion? You are a hero, shall I give you lessons in heroism and its vows?

Jivananda overwhelmed with joy said, "Still you have taught me!" With a happy heart Santi continued, "Also my lord, even in this life our marriage is not fruitless. "You love me. I love you. Is there in this life a greater boon? Sing — "Bande Mataram." Then both together sang

"Bande Mataram."

Chapter IV

BHAVANANDA Goswami one day went to the city. Leaving the broad main road he entered a narrow lane. On both sides of the lane were rows of high houses. Only at noon sometimes the sun shines in this lane. After that the darkness is greater. Bhavananda Thakur entered two-storied home on one side of the lane. He went to a room in the ground floor where a middle aged woman was cooking. She was middle aged, plump, dark, wearing a nose ring, her forehead tatooed, her hair bound in a knot at the top of her head. She was stirring the rice pot noisily striking the pot with the laddie, the straggling ends of her hair stirred by the breeze whilst she was going on speaking to herself with grimaces and shakes of the head which made the top knot on her head move in all directions. At this time Bhavananda Mahaprabhu entered the room and said, "Sister, accept my morning obeisance."

When the woman saw Bhavananda she began hastily to set right her disarranged clothes. She thought of undoing the top knot on her head and unloosing her hair, but she could not do so with her hands unclean from stirring the rice. That wet and shining hair, alas! at the time of doing poojah she had placed a Bak flower in it. She tried to hide it with the upper half of her cloth, but the cloth was unable to cover it because the woman was wearing a short cloth 2½ yds. in length only. That cloth of 2½ yds. after being wound round her ample girth was almost finished. Still it had tried to cover a portion of her heavy breasts. But reaching the shoulder it had given notice that it could not perform any further function. When she pulled it, reaching her ears it could reach no more. Resigned to the inevitable modest Gouri Devi held the cloth near her ears and swearing to herself in future buy a cloth at least 4 yds. in length said, "Who is it, — Goswami Thakur? Come! Come! But why do you offer morning obeisance to me, brother?

Bhavananda: Because you are my grand-dam.

Gouri: You say so in affection. But you are Goswamins — Gods, you know. All the same since you have offered your obeisance allow me to bless you with a long life. Besides you can offer your obeisance to me.

After all I am older.

Now, Bhavananda was at least 25 years younger than Gouri Devi, but clever Bhavananda replied, "What are you talking about, grand-dam? Because you can appreciate humour, I call you my grand-dam. Otherwise when we last compared our age you were found to be six years younger than me, don't you remember? As you know, there are all sorts of practices among us Vaishnavas. It is my desire to take the permission of the Brahmachari head of our Math and to many you. I came to tell you that."

Gouri: Fie. What an idea? You should never think of it. I am a widow.

Bhavananda: Then we cannot marry?

Gouri: Well then, brother, do as you think best. You are Pundits. We are mere women. What do we understand about these matters? Then when will it be?

Bhavananda with difficulty controlling his laughter said, "I have only to meet the Brahmachari fellow.......Well! How is she?"

Gouri became sad. She began to suspect that the proposal of marriage was a mere joke. She said, "How else can she be except just as usual?"

Bhavananda: Please go and see once how she is and tell her have come and shall see her.

Gouri Devi threw down the ladle with which she was stirring the rice and climbing the high steep stairs went to the 1st floor. On a torn mat was seated a wonderfully beautiful woman. But on her beauty a deep shadow seemed to lie. It was a shadow like that of a dark cloud cast over broad deep river with overflooded banks glittering in the midday sun. The waves were tossing in mid stream, on the banks the flowering trees were swaying with the breeze and bending under their floral load and the houses too were looking picturesque. The row of boats as they cut across the water left a trail of waves? It was mid-day, *yet* that dark cloudy shadow cast a gloom over all this beauty. It was the same here. There was the same lovely lustrous thick silken tresses, there was on the calm full forehead the same incomparable pencilled arched eyebrows, the same moist glistening bright black large eyes only without the same glamourous glances, without the same languishing look, just a little lowered. But there were the same crimson lips, there were the same full ripe breasts trembling with every breath, there were the same soft rounded arms which the creepers of the forest might envy. But today in that beauty there was not that brightness, that glitter, that shimmer, that charm. One might even say there did not seem to be the same youthfulness as before. There was only the same beauty and its innate sweetness. And to it was added a new quality — a patient gravity. Previously she appeared to be an incomparably beautiful woman in this world of human beings, but now she appeared to be a cursed Goddess in the abode of the Gods. Scattered about her were two or three manuscripts. On the wall was hung a rosary uttering Harinam and here and there paintings depicting Jagannath, Balaram and Subhadra, the overcoming of the demon Kaliya, Nabanarikunja, the stealing of the clothes of the Gopies at their bath by Krishna, the bearing on his hand the hill of Gobordhan by Krishna and other pictures relating to the Braja Lila, Some one had written under the pictures, — "Pictures or Wonders?" Bhavananda entered that room.

Bhavananda asked: Kalyani, are you well?

Kalyani: Will you not stop asking me the same question? What good can come from my physical well-being either to you or to me?

Bhavananda: He who plants a tree, each day he waters it. If the tree grows he is pleased. I planted life and vitality in your dead body. Whether that vitality is increasing or not, should I not ask?

Kalyani: Does the poison tree ever wither?

Bhavananda: Is life poison?

Kalyani: Otherwise why did I try to destroy it by pouring nectar into it?

Bhavananda: I have long desired to ask you the reason, but I had not the courage to ask. Who made your life poisonous?

Kalyani answered quite calmly, "No one made my life poisonous. Life itself is so — my life, your life, all our lives."

Bhavananda: Truly, Kalyani, my life is poisonous. Since the day...... Have you finished your Sanskrit grammar?

Kalyani: No.

Bhavananda: Your Sanskrit word book?

Kalyani: I do not like it.

Bhavananda: I saw you take some interest in your studies. Why this disgust now?

Kalyani: When a scholar like you is such a great sinner, then it is better not to study. My Lord, what news of my husband?

Bhavananda: Why do you repeatedly ask for news of him? For you he is as good as dead.

Kalyani: I am dead for him, not he for me.

Bhavananda: You died so that he should be dead to you. Then why harp on the same topic, Kalyani?

Kalyani: If one dies, does all relation cease? How is he?

Bhavananda: He is well.

Kalyani: Where is he? At Padachinha?

Bhavananda: Yes, he is there.

Kalyani: What is he doing?

Bhavananda: The same thing that he was doing — constructing a fort and manufacturing arms. With the arms he has manufactured thousands of Santans have been armed. Because of him we are not wanting in guns, shells, cartridges, gun-powder. Amongst the Santans he is indeed the most excellent. He has done us a great service. He is our right hand.

Kalyani: If I had not died, would all this have taken place? He round whose neck is tied a vessel full of mud, can he swim in the ocean of the world? He whose feet are chained, can he run? Why did I you preserve this vain life, Oh! Sannyasin?

Bhavananda: One's wife is the partner of one's religion, its support.

Kalyani: Yes, in small religions. But in great religions she is a thorn. By the thorn of poison I took out this thorn of irreligion. Fie on you. Oh sinful wicked Brahmacharin! Why did you revive this life?

Bhavananda: It is well. What I have given let it be mine. That life which was my gift can you give it to me?

Kalyani: Do you know how is my child Sukumari?

Bhavananda: For long I have had no news of her, Jivananda has not gone that way for long.

Kalyani: Can you bring me that news? I have given up my husband. But since I am alive, why should I abandon my child? If I can get Sukumari now, there is some possibility of getting a little joy in life. But why should you do so much for me?

Bhavananda: I shall do so, Kalyani. I shall bring your child to you. But after that?

Kalyani: After that? What do you mean, Thakur?

Bhavananda: Your husband?

Kalyani: Willingly I have given him up.

Bhavananda: If his vow is successfully fulfilled?

Kalyani: Then I shall be his. Does he know that I am alive?

Bhavananda: No!

Kalyani: Do you not meet him?

Bhavananda: I do.

Kalyani: Does He not speak about me?

Bhavananda: No, the wife who is dead what relationship can the husband have with her?

Kalyani: What are you talking about?

Bhavananda: You can marry again. You have been reborn.

Kalyani: Bring me my child.

Bhavananda: I shall do so. You can marry again.

Kalyani: Whom? You?

Bhavananda: Will you marry?

Kalyani: You?

Bhavananda: If that be so?

Kalyani: Where will your Santan religion be?

Bhavananda: It will be drowned in fathomless waters.

Kalyani: Your future life?

Bhavananda: That too will be drowned in fathomless waters.

Kalyani: This great vow?

Bhavananda: It will be drowned in fathomless waters too.

Kalyani: For what will you let all these be drowned in fathomless waters?

Bhavananda: For you. The heart is without control, whether it be that of a man, a saint — one who has attained fulfilment and release, or even if he be a God. The religion of the Santans is my very life. But for the first time I tell you today that you are dearer to me than my very life. From the day when I gifted you with life, from that day I sold myself as a slave at your feet. I did not know before that there was so much beauty in this world. Had I seen such beauty I would never have embraced the religion of the Santans. In the fire of your beauty my religion is burnt to ashes. My religion has been burnt, my life still remains. These four years my life too is being burnt in the fire of your beauty. It cannot be preserved any longer. It is a burning fire, Kalyani, but the wood which is to catch fire, that is gone. My life is ebbing away. For four years I have borne it. I can bear it no longer. Will you be mine?

Kalyani: I have heard from your own mouth that according to the religion of the Santans, he who is overcome by lust, his penance is death. Is this true?

Bhavananda; It is true.

Kalyani: Your penance then is death.

Bhavananda: My only penance is death.

Kalyani: If I fulfil your desire will you die?

Bhavananda: Certainly I shall die.

Kalyani: And if I do not fulfil your desire?

Bhavananda: Still death is my penance. Because my heart has become subject to my senses.

Kalyani: I shall not fulfil your desire. When will you die?

Bhavananda: In the next battle.

Kalyani: Then leave me. Will you send my child to me?

Bhavananda with tears in his eyes said, “I shall do so. When I die will you remember me?”

Kalyani: I shall do so but as a sinful breaker of vows.

Bhavananda went away. Kalyani sat down to read the manuscripts.

Chapter V

BHAVANANDA went towards the Math in deep meditation. It was night before he reached. He. was going alone on the road. He entered the forest alone. He saw that another person was walking in front of him. Bhavananda asked, "Who goes there?"

The person who was going in front said. "If properly asked I may reply — I am a traveller."

Bhavananda: Bande!

The person in front: "Mataram!"

Bhavananda: I am Bhavananda Goswami.

The person in front: "I am Dhirananda."

Bhavananda: Dhirananda, where have you been?

Dhirananda: Seeking you.

Bhavananda: Why?

Dhirananda: To tell you something.

Bhavananda: What?

Dhirananda: It can only be told in a lonely place.

Bhavananda: You can tell me here. This is a very lonely place.

Dhirananda: Did you go to the city?

Bhavananda: Yes!

Dhirananda: To the house of Gouri Devi?

Bhavananda: Did you go to the city also?

Dhirananda: A very beautiful woman dwells there?

Bhavananda was partly astonished and partly frightened. He "What is this you are saying?"

Dhirananda: You met her?

Bhavananda: What next?

Dhirananda: You are much attracted to that woman.

Bhavananda after thinking a bit said, "Dhirananda, why did you take such detailed information? Well, what you have said is all true. Besides you, how many people know this?

Dhirananda: None else.

Bhavananda: Then if I can kill you I can be free from the shame of possible exposure.

Dhirananda: That is so.

Bhavananda: Then come! In this lonely place let us both fight. Either I shall kill you and rid myself of a thorn, or you will kill me and cure me of all my pain. Have you got a weapon?

Dhirananda: I am armed — none would dare to say these things to you unarmed. If you insist in fighting I shall fight. Disputes between Santans are forbidden; but it is not forbidden to fight in self-defence. That which I was searching you for in order to tell you, would it not be better to hear it out before fighting?

Bhavananda: There is no harm, speak!

Bhavananda took his sword from its sheath and placed it on the shoulders of Dhirananda, so that he should not fly.

Dhirananda: I was just telling you this — why do you not marry Kalyani?

Bhavananda: It is Kalyani, you know that too?

Dhirananda: Why not marry her?

Bhavananda: She has a husband.

Dhirananda: Such marriages are possible amongst Vaishnavas.

Bhavananda: That is the case with mendicants and shaven-head Vaishnavas — not with Santans. Santans may not marry.

Dhirananda: The religion of the Santans may be abandoned. Your life is at stake. Fie! My shoulder is bleeding. (Really blood was dropping from Dhirananda's shoulders).

Bhavananda: What is the reason for which you have come to persuade me to follow the path of sin? Surely you have some motive in this.

Dhirananda: That too I wish to say. Don't dig your sword into my shoulder please. I am disgusted with this religion of the Santans. I wish to abandon it and am eager to see the faces of my wife and children and spend my days with them. I shall abandon this religion of the Santans. But it is impossible for me to stay in my house. Many know me to be a rebel. If I go home either the state officials will cut off my head or the Santans will kill me as a traitor and go away. This is why I wish to convert you into my way of thinking.

Bhavananda: Why me?

Dhirananda: That is the chief thing. The Santans are under your command. Satyananda is not here. You are their leader. Fight with these soldiers. You will win I am fully convinced. As soon as you win why not establish a kingdom in your own name? The army is under your command. Be a king. Let Kalyani be your Mandodari. I shall be your follower and spend the rest of my days seeing the faces of my wife and children, and in blessing you. Let the religion of the Santans be drowned in the deep sea.

Bhavananda slowly took the sword off Dhirananda's shoulder. He said, "Dhirananda! Fight, I shall kill you. I may be subject to my senses but I am not a traitor. You have advised me to be a traitor. You are yourself a traitor. To kill you will not amount to the sin of killing a Brahmin. I shall kill you."

But Dhirananda, before Bhavananda had finished speaking, ran for all he was worth. Bhavananda did not follow him. For a while Bhavananda became absent-minded. When he searched for him he could not find him.

Chapter VI

AFTER going to the Math Bhavananda entered into the depths of the forest. There was in one place a ruined house. Over the ruin and the stones thorns, shrubs and creepers had grown in thick luxuriance. There numberless snakes had made their home. One of these rooms in ruins was more or less whole and fairly clean. Bhavananda went and sat there. Having sat there he started thinking.

The night was pitch dark. To add to it, that forest was very large, absolutely uninhabited, very dense, the trees and creepers impenetrable, so that even wild animals scarcely penetrated there. It was a huge forest, uninhabited, dark impenetrable, silent — and in the distance the roaring of the tiger or the sounds of hungry, frightened or threatening wild animals were heard. Sometimes the flapping of the wings of some huge bird, and sometimes the sound of the flying feet of animals pursuing or being pursued could be heard. In that lonely darkness seated in the ruins, alone, was Bhavananda. For him the world was nonexistent or existed only in essence. He was seated, his head resting on his hand thinking, motionless, fearless, almost it seemed without breathing he remained immersed in deep thought. He was saying to himself — "What is destined, must be. Like a small elephant fallen into the waves of the mighty Ganges I am being carried away in the current of my senses. That is my sorrow. This moment, my body may be destroyed. The destruction of the body is the destruction of the senses. I have become the slave of those senses. It is better that I should die. I am a traitor to my religion. Fie! I shall die" Just then an owl overhead hooted loudly. Bhavananda then began to speak aloud. "What is that noise? It is as if I hear the God of death calling me. I know not who made the noise — who called me? Who gave me the orders? Who asked me to die? Oh Blessed Infinite! You are sound incarnate, but I do not understand the inner meaning of your sound. Lead me along the path of my religion, turn me away from sin. Oh my Guru! Let my mind be led along the path of religion!"

Then, from the forest an extremely sweet yet grave, an extremely tender touching human voice was heard. Some one said, "May your mind be led along the path of religion. I bless you."

Bhavananda's hairs stood on end. What was that! That was the voice of his guru. He cried aloud, — "Maharaj — where are you? Let your servant have sight of you at this time."

But no one showed himself. No one replied. Bhavananda called out repeatedly. He received no answer. He searched on all sides but no one was there.

When morning dawned and the sun rose lighting up that dense green foliage overhead of that great forest, Bhavananda returned to the Math. He could hear some one chanting. "Harrey Murarey!" He recognised Satyananda's voice. He understood that Satyananda had returned.

Chapter VII

WHEN Jivananda had left the hut Santi again took out the Sarang and began to sing softly:

In stormy oceans tempest tost
    You do float
    Like a boat
The Vedas in your self reposing
Effortless how dear enclosing.
Like a fish you take form
    Keshava sweet!
    Whilst, at your feet
Lord of the world! your praise we sing,
With praise of Hari the world doth ring.

When the sweet hymn of praise composed by the Goswami poet from the voice of Santi Devi clothed in the magic of musical notes and rhythmic cadence penetrated the infinite silence of the endless forest and came like the surge of waves of the blue ocean moved by the breezes of spring which breaks rhythmically on the shore, the sound became full and sweet; then she thus sang: —

Then compassionate to all creatures
    As Buddha great
    You do hate
Sacrificial rites of blood,
Creation with your love you flood.
Lord of the world your praise we sing,
With praise of Hari the world doth ring.

Then from outside some one sang in a voice deep as a roll of thunder,

"As Kalki incarnate you do come
    The barbaric herd
    With thy sword

Bright as a comet, Oh! to kill
The world with light how fair to fill.
Lord of the world your praise we sing,
With praise of Hari the world doth ring.

Santi full of devotion fell at the feet of Satyananda and took the dust of his feet. She said, "My Lord, for what good fortune is my home made sacred with the dust of your feet and why my eyes blessed with sight of you? Please tell me what I am to do. Saying this once more sweeping the cords of the Sarang with the bow she sang:

Lord your blessings no more delay,
    As at your feet
    Sacred sweet
For our welfare we do pray.

Satyananda said, "My daughter, good fortune will be yours."

Santi: How can that be when your orders to me are to embrace widowhood.

Satyananda: I did not know you then — my daughter not realising the strength of the rope I pulled too hard. You are wiser than me, it is for you to find some way out. Do not tell Jivananda that I know everything. For your sake he can preserve his life. He is doing so till now. Then alone can my work be accomplished.

Over those flashing black eyes an angry glance played as the lightening plays in the dark summer clouds. Santi said, "How can that be, my lord! My husband and I are one soul. Whatever has passed between you and me I shall tell him all. If he is to die, he will die. It is no loss to me. I too shall die with him. If heaven be his reward do you think I too shall not go to heaven?

The Brahmacharin said, "I have never been defeated. Today I acknowledge defeat by you. My daughter, I am like your son. Have compassion on your child. Save Jivananda. Save your own life. Accomplish my work."

Santi's smile flashed out like lightening. "My husband's religion is his own concern. Who am I to take him from the path of his religion? In this life, to a woman, her husband is a god, but in the life to come to us all, our religion is our God. To me my husband is great, but my religion is greater, but greater still than that is the religion of my husband. I can sacrifice my religion whenever I so desire. But shall I sacrifice my husband's religion? At your command if my husband has to die let him die. I shall not ask him to live."

The Brahmacharin sighed deeply and said, "My daughter, in this terrible vow sacrifice is essential. We must all offer ourselves as a sacrifice. I shall die. Jivananda, Bhavananda, each must die. Most probably you too will die. But my daughter, we must accomplish our work before death. To die without accomplishing our work, is that desirable? I have only called the country my mother. I acknowledge no other mother because except this well-watered fruitful Motherland we have no other mother. I call upon you as my mother. Be a mother and do the work of your child. Do that which will accomplish our work, save Jivananda's life, save your own life." Saying these words Satyananda chanting "O Hari! O Murari!" O Slayer of Madhu and Kaitava, left the place.

Chapter VIII

GRADUALLY the news spread amongst the Santans that Satyananda had come and wished to speak to the Santans. He had called them. Then in groups the Santans began to collect. It was a moonlit night. Near the bank of the river in the huge forest under the shade of mangoes, jackfruits, palms, banyans, tamarinds, Baels, Bata and Salmali trees ten thousand Santans gathered. Then all hearing from each other of the arrival of Satyananda sent up an uproar in joy. They did not know where and for what purpose Satyananda had gone. The rumour was that he had gone to the Himalayas for practicing austerities for the welfare of the Santans. Thus today all the Santans started saying to each other, "Our Guru has been successful in his mission. We shall win, the kingdom will be ours." Soon there was great shoutings. Some cried, "Kill the Mussulmans!" Some shouted, "Victory for our Guru" Some sang — "Bande Mataram" and others "O Hari! O Murari" etc. Some said, "Brother, will the day dawn when being mere Bengalees we shall be able to die in the battlefield?" Some said, "Brother will the day dawn when destroying Masjids we shall be able to establish there temples of Radhamadhava?" Some said, "Brother, will the day dawn when we shall be able to enjoy our own produce and riches?" Ten thousand human voices mingled with the rustling in sweet breeze of the innumerable leaves of trees, and the murmur of the waves of the river flowing between beaches; whilst all around was the verdant earth, the green forest, the flowery groves and the white sands of the riverside and above, in the blue sky the moon, the stars and the fleecy white clouds. Amongst all these burst out now and then that most beautiful of sounds — "Bande Mataram."

Satyananda came and stood amidst that gathering of Santans. Then those ten thousand Santans bent their heads on the green ground — heads lighted with moon-light coming through the interstices of the leaves. In a loud voice with tearful eyes raising both his hands high over his head Satyananda said, "One who wields and holds the conch shell, the disc, the club and the lotus, Banamali, the Lord of heaven, one who destroyed Kesi, Madhu, Mura and Naraka, who is the preserver of this world, may He bring you wellbeing, may He give strength to your arms, devotion to your heart and urge you towards religion. Come one and all and sing His glory. Then in those thousand voices was sung loudly,—

Lord of the world thy praise we sing,
With praise of Hari the world doth ring!
In stormy ocean tempest-tost
  You do float
  Like a boat;
The Vedas in yourself reposing
Effortless how dear enclosing —
Like a fish you take form.
  Keshava sweet!
  Whilst at your feet,
Lord of the world your praise we sing —
With praise of Hari the world doth ring.

Satyananda again blessing them said, "Oh Santans! I have something very particular to tell you today. One Thomas by name, an irreligious and bad-hearted man has destroyed many Santans. Tonight we shall kill him and wipe out his army. This is the Will of God — what do you say?"

A terrible shout of "Hari Hari" pierced the forest. "We shall kill him just now. Where are they? Come and show us. Kill! Kill our enemies!" — this cry echoed back from the distant hill. Then Satyananda said, "For that we have got to hold our soul in patience for a while The enemies? possess guns — without guns fighting against them is hardly possible. Moreover they are a race of heroes. There are seventeen cannons being brought from the fort of Padachinha, as soon as they arrive we shall start on our war-path. Just look, the dawn is breaking.... What is that?"

Booming of cannons! Suddenly in that huge mango-grove guns were booming. They were British guns. Captain Thomas had surrounded the grove in order to kill the entire Santan body like fish caught in a net.

Chapter IX

WITH deep booming sound the British guns roared. Shaking that vast forest, the sound echoed in a fresh booming. Moving along the embankment of the river it was thrown back again from the distant horizon. Crossing the river and penetrating the further woods the boom of the guns called again, Satyananda ordered them, "Go and find out whose are those guns." Some of the Santans rushed forward on horse back to reconnoitre. But as soon as they, emerging from the forest, had proceeded some distance, cannon balls were showered on them like rain, all of them got wounded along with their horses and died. Satyananda saw it from a distance. He said, "Climb a high tree and find out what it is." But before he said it Jivananda had climbed up a tree and was looking about him in the morning light He shouted down from the top of the tree, "The guns belong to the British." Satyananda asked. "Are these cavalry or infantry?"

Jivananda: Both are there.

Satyananda: How many?

Jivananda: I cannot guess as they are still emerging from the forest.

Satyananda: Are there British troops, or only Sepahis?

Jivananda: There are British troops alright.

Satyananda told Jivananda, "You get down from the tree." Jivananda got down. Satyananda said, "There are ten thousand Santans present. Try and see what you can do with them. You are the general today." Jivananda armed himself well and jumped on his horse. Once be looked at Nabinananda and some signal passed between them which no one else understood. Nabinananda too answered through look, which also none could comprehend. Only both of them realised, that, very possibly they were parting for good. At that time Nabinananda raising his right hand said to all, "Brothers, let us sing now, "All glory to Jagadish Hare." Then those ten thousand Santans with raised hands sang in one voice resounding with their song the river, forest and sky and drowning the boom of the guns in it —

Lord of the world thy praise we sing
With praise of Hari the world doth ring.
The barbaric horde
With thy sword —
Oh to kill!

Just then the shell of the British guns began raining on the Santans in the forest. Some of them fell down singing decapitated, some handless, others with their heart ripped open. Even then none stopped singing. All sang together, "Glory to Jagadisha Hare."

When the song was concluded all was silent.

That dense forest, that river bank, that lonely region all became steeped in deep silence; there was only heard that distant and terrible roar of the guns, clatter of weapons of the British troops and the sound of their footsteps.

Then Satyananda broke that stillness and shouted in a loud voice, "Hari the Lord of the universe has taken compassion on you — How far are the guns?"

Some one answered from above, "Very near this forest on the other side of a small field."

Satyananda asked, "Who are you?"

The answer came from above, "I am Nabinananda."

Then Satyananda said, "You Santans are ten thousand in number, victory will surely come to you today, go and seize the gun." Then Jivananda on horseback in front of them cried, "Come on!"

Those ten thousand Santans — both infantry and cavalry followed Jivananda at a rush. The fighters on foot carried their guns on their shoulders, a sword at their waist and a lance in their hands. As soon as they emerged from the forest the shower of cannon balls fell on them and dispersed them. Many Santans lay on the ground dead without a chance of fighting. Some one said to Jivananda, "Jivananda, of what use is this waste of human life?"

Jivananda turned and found that that person was Bhavananda. Jivananda asked, "What do you advise me to do?"

Bhavananda: Let us remain in the forest and save our lives under the cover of trees. In the open field in the face of guns and without support of our guns this Santan army cannot expect to stand for a moment. But behind bushes we can carry on the fight for a long time.

Jivananda: What you say is true, but our Master has ordered us to seize the gun, so we shall proceed to do it.

Bhavananda: Who can possibly seize it? But if some one must do it, you desist, I shall go forward.

Jivananda: That won't do, Bhavananda. I have got to die today.

Bhavananda: I have go to die today too.

Jivananda: I have to atone for my sin.

Bhavananda: You are untouched by sin, you have no need for atonement. My heart is unclean — it is I who have got to die. You remain behind, I go.

Jivananda: Bhavananda, what sin you may have committed, I don't know; but if you live, the purpose of the Santans will be served. Let me go instead.

Bhavananda keeping quiet for a time said, "If dying is in question we may die today, or on any other day if we are required to do so as well. Need we look for an auspicious moment for dying?

Jivananda: Then come along.

After this parley Bhavananda kept himself in front. Just then cannon balls in spurts and showers were falling on the Santan force breaking them, tearing them, tossing them up; over and above that the Sepahis' muskets with their unerring aim were shooting down rank after rank of Santans. At that moment Bhavananda said, "We have got to jump in this deadly current, brothers, which of you dare? Now come let us sing "Bande Mataram!" Then in full throated chorus in loud Megha-mallar tune keeping time with the boom of cannons the Santan army sang "Hail Mother!"

Chapter X

THOSE ten thousand Santans rushed forward with their lances raised singing "Hail Mother" all the time and thus fell on the guns placed in a line. They were cut to pieces, some of their bodies ripped open, tumbled about, and all of them were disorganised, but in spite of it the Santan troops would not turn back. Just at that moment, ordered by Captain Thomas, a party of Sepahis with fixed bayonet attacked the right flank of the Santans with great force. Thus attacked from two sides the Santans became down-hearted. Every minute hundreds of them were being killed. Then Jivananda said, "Bhavananda, you are right; this destruction of Vaishnabas need not continue, let us fall back slowly."

Bhavananda: How can you turn back now? Whoever will try now to turn back will surely die.

Jivananda: The attack is coming from the front as well as from the right. There is no one on the left, come, let us slowly wheel to the left and slip away.

Bhavananda: Where will you slip away? There is the river on that side — rains have helped to swell it immensely. You propose to run away from the guns of the British and help to drown the Santan army in the river?

Jivananda: I seem to remember, that, there is a bridge on the river.

Bhavananda: To attempt to take across ten thousand Santan soldiers over that bridge will result in such a packed crowd that, perhaps one single gun will be enough to destroy the entire army.

Jivananda: Do one thing, keep a handful of soldiers and hold the front — the courage and skill in tactics that you have shown in this battle, shows that there is nothing which you cannot do. You hold the front with that small band of Santans. Behind the screen of your fighters let me try and take the rest of the Santan army across the bridge. Those who are left with you will meet sure death, while those who are with me may escape destruction.

Bhavananda: Alright, I am doing what you suggest.

Then Bhavananda taking two thousand Santans with him and raising the shout of "Hail Mother" again attacked the gunners of the British with great energy. A great battle raged there. But how long can a small band of Santans last in the face of blazing guns? The gunners began cutting them down like paddy reaped with scythes.

Availing himself of this opportunity Jivananda turning the front of his remaining Santans a little and wheeling behind the forest to the left began slowly to retreat.

Captain Thomas's fellow officer Lieutenant Watson noticed from a distance, that, a part of the Santan force was fleeing by degrees; he followed Jivananda with a band of Fouzdari Sepahis and another band of Purgana Sepahis.

All these movements were observed by Captain Thomas. Seeing that the main Santan force was running away he told a fellow officer Captain Hay, "With three or four hundreds of soldiers I am cutting down these broken up rebels, you take the rest of the force and the guns and rush after them. Lieutenant Watson is following them from the left, you go after them from the right, and look here, you will have to be there first to close up the outlet in the bridge, then we shall be able to kill them out like birds caught in a net. They are swift-footed native soldiers, they are great adepts in running away only; so you will not be able to catch them up easily. You tell the cavalry to proceed under cover making long circuit for the bridge mouth and take up position there, then our object will be gained." Captain Hay carried this out.

Excessive pride was the cause of the destruction of Lanka (the golden city of Ravan in the Ramayan). Captain Thomas having great contempt for the Santans, kept back only two hundred men for his fight with Bhavananda sending the rest away with Captain Hay. When shrewd Bhavananda saw that all the guns of the British had left, the major part of their force was gone too, the handful of men left behind was easy to destroy, he called the Santans about him who had escaped carnage and said, "I have to go to Jivananda's help after killing these few men. Once again cry "Glory to Jagadisha Hare!" Then with the battle cry of "Glory to Jagadisha Hare" that small band of Santans leapt on Captain Thomas and his men like tigers. The handful of Tailangi Sepahis could not stand against that furious onslaught, they were wiped out. Bhavananda then went himself and caught hold of Captain Thomas by the hair. Captain Thomas was fighting on up to the last. Bhavananda said, "Captain Sahib, I shall not kill you, the English are not our enemies. Why have you come to the aid of the Mussulmans? Come, I give you back your forfeited life. For the present you are our prisoner. Victory to the British! We are your friends."

Captain Thomas then tried to raise his gun with bayonet fixed with the intention of killing Bhavananda, but Bhavananda had caught him in the grip of a tiger, so Captain Thomas could not move. Then Bhavananda ordered his men, "Tie him up." Two to three of the Santans came and bound Captain Thomas. Bhavananda said, "Put him on a horse, and come, let us go to Jivananda Goswami's help."

Then that small body of Santans taking Captain Thomas bound hand and foot on a horse with them and singing "Hail Mother" dashed forward with Watson as their objective.

The demoralised Santan force under Jivananda was about to run away. Jivananda and Dhirananda somehow persuaded and kept them restrained, but could not induce all to stay, some of them fled and took cover in the mango grove. Jivananda and Dhirananda led the rest of them to the mouth of the bridge. There Hay and Watson surrounded them from two sides. Their situation became pretty hopeless.

Chapter XI

JUST then the guns of Captain Thomas appeared in the south. Then the Santans began indeed to be cut up, there was no hope left of anybody escaping. They began to run away wherever they could, Jivananda and Dhirananda tried their level best to restrain and hold them together, but could not succeed at all. At that moment a loud cry was heard — "Go to the bridge, manoeuvre towards the bridge!"

Jivananda looked that way and found Bhavananda in front of him. Bhavananda said, "Take them to the bridge, there is no hope of escape now."

Then slowly the Santan force began falling backward to the direction of the bridge. But as reaching the bridge many Santans began pouring across it, the British guns availing themselves of this opportunity literally began sweeping the bridge with their guns. The Santans began to be annihilated. Bhavananda, Jivananda and Dhirananda met together. One particular gun was the cause of loss of a large number of Santans. Bhavananda said, "Jivananda and Dhirananda! Come on, with the sweep of our swords let us capture this gun." Then all the three whirling their swords cut down all gunners near it. More and more Santans came to their help. The gun was captured by Bhavananda, Taking possession of it Bhavananda stood up on it. He clapped his hands and said, "Sing — Hail Mother!" They all sang "Hail Mother!" Bhavananda said, "Jivananda, let us turn this gun against them and let us pound them into wheat flour good enough for preparing *loochis*." The Santans took hold of the gun and reversed it. Then the gun began roaring as it were the name of Hari to the ear of the Vaishnabas. Many Sepahis began to get killed with its help. Bhavananda dragged the gun forward and placing it at the mouth of the bridge said, "Both of you take the Santan army across the bridge in a line, I shall alone protect the bridge head. Leave with me a few gunners to fire the gun." Twenty picked Santans remained by Bhavananda's side.

Then by the order of Jivananda and Dhirananda countless Santans began reaching the other side of the river crossing the bridge in an unbroken row. Single-handed Bhavananda, aided by those twenty

Santans, destroyed any number of soldiers with the help of that isolated gun. But those *Javana* hordes were like the surge of waves. Wave after wave, wave after wave — they surrounded Bhavananda, oppressed and almost drowned him. Bhavananda, tireless, unconquerable and fearless, went on killing numerous soldiers at every burst of his gun. The Mussulman hordes like storm-driven waves went on attacking him, but those twenty Santans with their gun kept the bridge head successfully sealed. They refused to get wiped out — the Mussulmans could not get on the bridge. Those heroes were unconquerable, those lives were immortal. Availing themselves of this opportunity band after band of Santans crossed over to the opposite bank. Given some time more and the bridge thus protected, all the Santans could safely go across the bridge; just at that moment from somewhere new guns began sending out boom after boom, roar after roar. Both sides ceased fighting for a time and looked about themselves for the whereabouts of these guns. They saw that several guns led by Indian gunners were emerging out of the forest. Coming out of the woods this huge row of guns belching smoke from their seventeen muzzles began showering fire on Hay's troops. Forest and hills echoed back that fearful din. Mussulman hordes tired out by the day-long fighting began trembling for fear of their life. Before that shower of flame Mussulmans and Hindusthanis began to run away. Only isolated British soldiers stood their ground and died on the spot.

Bhavananda was witnessing the fun. He said, "Brother, the Mussulmans are taking to their heels, come, let us attack them." Then with renewed energy, just like swarms of ants, the Santans recrossed the bridge and rushed to attack the Mussulmans; they fell suddenly on them. The Mohammedans had hardly any opportunity or time to fight, just as the currents of the Bhagirathi had swept away that mountain-like huge proud mad elephant, so the Santans swept the Mussulmans away. The Mussulmans found the infantry of Bhavananda behind them and Mohendra's guns in front. Then Hay Sahib's total destruction set in. Nothing stood that test; strength, courage, heroism, tactics, training, pride all were of no use. The troops imperial, of the Fouzdar, the British, Indian, black and white all lay on the ground. The irreligious bands of Heathens fled. With the cry "Kill — kill!" Jivananda, Dhirananda pursued the impious hordes. The Santans snatched away their guns.

Many British and Indian troops were killed. Facing every possibility of total destruction Captain Hay and Watson sent word to Bhavananda, "We are all willing to be your prisoners, don't destroy human life anymore." Jivananda looked at Bhavananda. Bhavananda said to himself, "That won't do, I have got to die today." Then Bhavananda raising his hands and uttering the name of Hari cried out in aloud voice, "Kill! kill!"

Not a single man escaped. At last at one spot twenty to thirty Britishers gathered and deciding to give themselves up fought on desperately. Jivananda said, "Bhavananda, we have become victorious, no use fighting any more, except this handful no one else is alive, let them go and let us return." Bhavananda said, "So long as a single man is alive Bhavananda will not return. Jivananda, upon God, I request you to stand aside and watch me kill these Englishmen single handed."

Captain Thomas was tied hand and foot on a horse. Bhavananda ordered, "Place that fellow in front of me, first he will die, only then will come my turn."

Captain Thomas understood Bengali, grasping the trend of what was said he cried out to the English soldiers present there, "Englishmen! I am as good as dead. You must preserve the honour of old England unsullied. Upon Christ, I tell you to kill me first and then kill these rebels."

A bullet whistled by, an Irishman having aimed at Captain Thomas and fired. Hit on his forehead Captain Thomas fell dead. Then Bhavananda called out, "My chief weapon of offence has failed. Are there any heroes like Bhima, Nakula and Sahadeva who will protect me? Look, like tigers wounded with arrows British soldiers are turning on me. I have come to die, is there any Santan here who is willing to die with me?"

First Dhirananda came forward, then followed Jivananda. Then came ten, fifteen, twenty, fifty Santans. Seeing Dhirananda Bhavananda asked, "You too come to die with us?"

Dhirananda: "Why, is dying anyone's monopoly?" Saying this Dhirananda wounded a British soldier.

Bhavananda: It's not that. But if you die you cannot expect to look at the dear faces of your wife and children and so spend your days in happiness!

Dhirananda: You are talking of yesterday. Have you not understood yet?

Dhirananda killed the wounded Britisher.

Bhavananda said, "No."

At this moment Bhavananda's right hand was cut off by a British soldier.

Dhirananda: How could I utter such things before you who are so pure-hearted. I went to you as a spy from Satyananda.

Bhavananda: What? Maharaja has lost his confidence in me?

Bhavananda was then fighting with his remaining hand. Dhirananda went on protecting him and said, "He had heard with his own ears your conversation with Kalyani."

Bhavananda: How?

Dhirananda: He was himself present there — Take care! (Being wounded by an Englishman Bhavananda returned his blow) — He was teaching Geeta to Kalyani when you appeared. Take care! (Bhavananda's left hand was severed).

Bhavananda: Please convey to him the news of my death. Tell him, I was not faithless.

Dhirananda fighting all the time said with tearful eyes, "He knows that. Remember the words of blessing uttered last night. Moreover he told me, "Remain near Bhavananda, he will die today. At the moment of his death, tell him, I am blessing him. In the other world he will reach heaven."

Bhavananda said, "Brother, may victory come to the Santans. At the time of my death sing 'Hail Mother'!"

Then ordered by Dhirananda all the Santans mad with lust of battle sang forcefully "Hail Mother!" That increased the strength in their arms twofold. At that terrible moment all the white men were killed. The battle field became quiet.

Just then with 'Hail Mother' on his lips and meditating on the feet of Vishnu Bhavananda died.

Fie! beauty and charm, of woman! You are accursed in this world.

Chapter XII

AFTER victory in battle, on the bank of the river Ajoy the victorious heroes rejoiced in various festivities. Only Satyananda mourned for Bhavananda.

So long the Vaishnavas had hardly any war band but at that moment from somewhere appeared thousands of Kara, Nagra, native drums. Kansi, Sanai, Turi, Veri, Ramsinga and Damama. The woods, fields and rivers began to echo and resound with this war-band denoting victory. When for a long time the Santans had rejoiced in festivities Satyananda said, "You have received God's grace today, the Santan religion is crowned with victory; but duty still remains unaccomplished. Those who cannot rejoice with us today, those who have offered their lives in order to make this festivity possible, we must not forget them. Let us go and perform the last rites for those who are lying dead on the battle-field. Specially that saintly person Bhavananda who has, for our sake, given up his life in battle, let us perform his funeral rites with great pomp and ceremony. Then with the cry — "Hail Mother," the Santans went to perform these rites for the dead. Many people assembled and with "Hari Bole" on their lips gathering sandal wood in heaps they built Bhavananda's funeral pyre, placing Bhavananda's body on it and setting fire to it they went round it again and again singing, "O Hari, O Murari" all the time. They were devotees of Vishnu, they did not really belong to the Vaishnava sect, so their custom was to cremate their dead bodies.

After that Satyananda, Jivananda, Mohendra, Nabinananda and Dhirananda sat together in the forest; they were busy in secret consultation. Satyananda said, "The vow for the sake of which we had so long renounced all avocations, all religion, all the pleasures of life, that vow stands fulfilled; there are no Mussulman soldiers left in this part of the country, what is left of the enemy they are not powerful enough to stand against us for an hour. What is your suggestion now?"

Jivananda said, "Let us go and occupy the capital."

Satyananda: I am of the same opinion.

Dhirananda: Where are soldiers?

Jivananda: Why, these are our soldiers.

Dhirananda: Where are the soldiers you talk of? Whom do you find here?

Jivananda: They must be resting here and there, if we beat the drum they will collect all right.

Dhirananda: You will not get a single one of them.

Satyananda: Why?

Dhirananda: All have gone out with the object of plunder. The villages are now unprotected. They will all go home after plundering the Mussulman villages and the silk factories. You will not get any one now, I have gone and made a search everywhere.

Satyananda became dejected; he said, whatever it is, this entire region is now under our occupation. There are none hereabout who can aspire to be our competitor. So you go about and proclaim the fact that there is Santan kingdom established in Barendra land, collect dues from the subjects and gather and organise soldiers for taking possession of the capital. If they hear that the Hindus have got their own kingdom, any number of soldiers will raise our flag."

Then Jivananda and others doing obeisance to Satyananda said, "We bow down to you, O King of Kings! If you order we can put up your throne in this very forest."

Satyananda for the first time in his life showed anger. He said, "Shame! You take me for an empty vessel! We are none of us rulers, we are all Sanyasins. No, the King of Heaven is himself our ruler. When the capital is occupied, you may put the crown on anybody's head you like, but know this much for certain that I shall acknowledge no other life than that of a Brahmachari. Now you can go about your business."

Then all four of them bowed to the Brahmachari; and got up. Satyananda unobserved by others signed to Mohendra and detained him. Three of them left. Mohendra stayed behind. Then Satyananda said to Mohendra, "All of you had taken the vow of the Santan religion on sacred oath in the Vishnu temple. Both Bhavananda and Jivananda transgressed their vow. Bhavananda has today gone through his agreed atonement. I am always on the tenter hooks of fear, that, some day Jivananda too may give up his body for atonement. But I have one consolation, for some secret reason he will not be able to die just at present. You alone have kept your vow inviolate. Now the object of the Santans is achieved. This was your vow, that so long as the purpose of the Santans is not fulfilled you will not look upon the faces of your wife and daughter. The object of the Santans is attained, now you can again go back to your householder's life."

Tears flowed from Mohendra's eyes copiously. Mohendra said, "My lord, with whom shall I begin my life as a householder? My wife committed suicide, and I don't know the whereabouts of my daughter. Where shall I get a clue to her? You have told me that she is alive, that much I know, I don't know anything beyond that."

Satyananda then called Nabinananda and said to Mohendra, "This is Nabinananda Goswami, he is pure-hearted and is my dearest disciple. He will give you the necessary clue to your daughter." Saying this Satyananda made some signs to Santi. Taking the hint Santi bowed to him and was on the point of leaving. Then Mohendra asked, "Where shall I meet you?"

Santi replied, "Come to my hermitage." Saying this Santi preceded him.

Then Mohendra making his obeisance to the Brahmachari took leave of him and followed Santi to her hermitage. It was late at night. Even then without taking rest Santi started for the town.

After all had left, the Brahmachari now alone bowed down his head on the ground and began meditating on God. Dawn was breaking. Just then some one came and touching his head said, "I have come."

The Brahmachari got up started and said eagerly, "Have you come? Why?"

The one who had come said, "The appointed time is completed."

The Brahmachari said, "O my lord! Excuse me today. On the next full-moon day in the month of Magh I shall do what you require of me."

PART IV

Chapter I

THAT night the whole region was ringing with cries of "Hari Hari!" The Santans roamed about in bands some singing "Hail Mother" and some "Jagadisha Hare." One party would take away the weapons of the enemies, others would remove their clothes. Some would kick at the face of the dead and others would do some other mischief. A few ran towards the village, others towards the town; they got hold of men on the streets and householders and said, "Sing 'Hail Mother' or we kill you." Some of them looted the sweetmeat shops, some entered milkmen's houses, took down vessels of curd and drank them up. Some said, "We are *Gopas* from *Braja,* where are the Gopinis?" In that single night there was an uproar in all the surrounding villages and towns. All began to say, "The Mussulmans are defeated, the country again belongs to the Hindus, let us all cry heartily 'Hari Hari'." The villagers began chasing the Mussulmans wherever they met them. Some banded themselves together, went to the Muslim quarters, set fire to their cottages and looted their all. Many Mussulmans were killed, many shaved off their beards, smeared themselves with Ganges clay and began singing "Hari Hari." If asked they said, "I am a Hindu."

Panic stricken Mussulmans in crowds began running towards the town. The Government officers rushed about and the remaining Sepahis armed themselves and stood in serried ranks for the defence of the town. On the rampart of the town in all the exits sentries stood carefully guarding the doors. People kept awake all night in anxiety not knowing what might happen any moment. The Hindus kept saying, "Let the Sannyasis come. May Mother Durga so ordain. Let that great day for the Hindus dawn at last." The Mussulmans kept saying, "Alla-ho-Akber! After such a long time the sayings of the Koran came to naught! We who pray to God five times a day could not defeat the Hindus who paste their brow with sandal wood paste! The world indeed an illusion!"

Thus some weeping, some rejoicing, the night was passed in eager expectations.

Kalyani heard all this talk. From a child to an old man all knew what was going on. Kalyani said to herself, "O God, your work is done at last. I shall start today to meet my husband. O Madhusudan! Come to my help today."

At dead of night Kalyani leaving her bed opened the back door and looked about her. Finding no one any where she left Gouri Devi's abode quietly and stepped into the road. She inwardly prayed to her God, "O Lord, ordain so that I may meet him at Padachinha today."

Kalyani reached the main gate of the town. The sentry called out, "Who goes there?" In a timid voice Kalyani answered, "I am only a woman." The sentry replied "There is no permission for anybody to go out." The Dafadar heard this and said, "There is no bar against going out. The order is against anybody entering the town." Hearing this the sentry said, "Go mother, there is no order against going out, But tonight it is not safe anywhere, I don't know whether you will fall into the hands of dacoits or into a ditch. Mother, please don't go out tonight"

Kalyani said, "My child! I am only a beggar woman. I have got not even a farthing with me. The dacoits will not touch me."

The sentry said, "You are young, mother, there is youth in you, that is riches indeed. Even I may turn out to be a dacoit for the sake of that."

Kalyani saw, there was danger here, without saying anything she quietly slipped past the town gate. The sentry finding her unappreciative of his humour took a long pull at his *ganja* and began singing a *tappa* song in *Jhinjhit Khambaj* tune. Kalyani went away.

That night, some wayfarers were shouting, "Kill them, kill them," others were crying out, "Run away, run away." Some were weeping, some laughing. Any body who met another chased him. Kalyani was in great difficulties. She did not remember the way, she could not ask anybody, all were in a militant mood. She had to proceed hiding herself in darkness. Even thus proceeding she fell in the hands of a lot of fierce rebels, They cried aloud and rushed to get hold of Her. Kalyani ran hard and entered a thick jungle. One or two dacoits followed her there even. One caught hold of her *sari* and said, "Now my moon!" Just then somebody appeared there suddenly and hit the tormentor with a stick. He fell back hurt. This rescuer was in a Sannyasi's garb, he had his bosom covered with a dark deer-skin. He was quite young in age. He said to

Kalyani. "Don't fear, come with me. Where will you go?"

Kalyani: To Padachinha.

The stranger was startled and surprised; he said, "What? — to Padachinha?" So saying the stranger placed both hands on the shoulders of Kalyani and began scrutinising her face carefully.

At the touch of a strange man Kalyani was amazed, nonplussed, terrified and tearful. She could hardly run away as she was helpless with fear. Finishing his scrutiny the stranger said, "O Hari! O Murari! I recognise you, you are Kalyani, the burnt-face!"

Kalyani timorously said, "Who are you."

The stranger replied, "I am the slave of your slave. O my beauty, come, be agreeable to me."

Kalyani quickly moved away and cried out in anger, "Did you save me only to insult me thus? I find you in the garb of a Brahmachari, is this the way a Brahmachari is expected to behave? Today I am helpless or I would have kicked at your face."

The Brahmachari said, "I have been long yearning for the touch of that beautiful body, O my smiling beauty!" Saying this the Brahmachari rushed at her, caught hold of her and embraced her ardently.

Then Kalyani laughed aloud and said, "O Lord! Why did you not tell me before that you were in the same plight as I?"

Santi said; "My sister! you are going to look for Mohendra?"

Kalyani asked, "Who are you? You seem to know everything!"

Santi said, "I am a Brahmachari. I am a leader of the Santans, a great hero! I know everything. Today the roads are beset and unsafe because of the Santans and the Sepahis. You cannot expect to go to Padachinha today."

Kalyani began weeping.

Santi rolled her eyes and said, "Why do you fear? We kill thousand enemies with the arrows of our amorous glances. Come, let us go to Padachinha.

Kalyani thought it a godsend to have the help of such a clever woman. She said, "I shall go wherever you take me."

Santi then took her and proceeded by a jungle path.

Chapter II

WHEN Santi left the Asram at the dead of night and started for the city Jivananda was present there. Santi told Jivananda, "I am going to the city. I shall fetch Mohendra's wife. Acquaint Mohendra with the fact, that, his wife is living."

Jivananda had heard from Bhavananda how Kalyani's life was saved and knew the present whereabouts of Kalyani from Santi who was in the habit of wandering every where. He began to acquaint Mohendra with every detail.

At first Mohendra could not believe it. Then he was overwhelmed with joy and almost stunned with it.

When the night was over Kalyani met Mohendra with Santi's help. In the silent forest under the dense thickly grown *sal* trees before the wild birds and animals awoke, the two met together. The only witness of this meeting were the dim stars in the blue sky and the hushed and endless *sal* trees. From a distance came the sweet voice of a narrow stream murmuring among stones and pebbles and the glad cry of a cuckoo beside itself with joy at the sight of the luminous crown of the rising sun in the east.

It was one hour past noon. Santi was there. Jivananda also came there. Kalyani said to Santi, "You have made us as good as your purchased slaves. Complete your good deed by letting us know the whereabouts of our daughter."

Santi looked at Jivananda's face and said, "I must sleep now. I have not rested in the last twenty-four hours. I have not slept for two nights — I am a man, after all.

Kalyani smiled a little. Jivananda looked at Mohendra's face said, "Leave that to me. You proceed to Padachinha — you will get your daughter there."

Jivananda went to Bharuipur to take away the child from Nimai — the thing was not so easy it seemed.

Nimai at first stood nonplussed; she looked this way and that. Her nostrils quivered and her lips were pursed up. Then she burst into tears. She declared, "I won't let you have the child."

After Nimai had dried her tears with the back of her supple rounded hand Jivananda said. "My sister, why do you weep? It is not so far off after all; you may visit them now and then at their house and see the child."

Nimai pursed her lips and said, "She is your child, take her away for all I care," Saying this she brought Sukumari, dumped her down there and squatting on the ground and stretching her feet started weeping. So Jivananda did not say anything about the matter but went on talking on casual topics. But Nimai's ruffled temper was not soothed. Nimai got up, began fetching Sukumari's bundle of clothes, her box of ornaments, her ribbons, her toys and threw them before Jivananda. Sukumari herself began collecting and arranging them. She began asking Nimai, "O mamma! where shall I go?" Nimai could not bear it any more. She picked the child up and went away weeping.

Chapter III

IN the newly constructed fort at Padachinha Mohendra, Kalyani, Jivananda, Santi, Nimai, Nimai's husband and Sukumari all happily met together, Santi had come in the guise of Nabinananda. The night she had brought Kalyani to her cottage, she forbade her to disclose the fact to her husband that Nabinananda was in reality a woman. On a certain day Kalyani sent for her. Nabinananda entered the inner precincts of the house. He did not listen to the dissuasions of the servants.

Santi came to Kalyani and asked, "Why have you called me?"

Kalyani: How long you will remain disguised as a man? I cannot talk with you — we can hardly meet. You must reveal your identity to my husband.

Nabinananda remained buried in deep thought, he did not speak for a long time. He said at last, "Kalyani, there are many difficulties in the way of that."

Both of them were busy talking about the matter. In the meantime the servants who had failed to dissuade Nabinananda from entering the inner precincts of the house went and reported to Mohendra, that, Nabinananda forced his way to the inner chambers and did not listen to their protests. Mohendra became curious and entered the inner precincts. Going into the bed room of Kalyani he found Nabinananda standing inside, Kalyani was standing near him, touching him and untying the knot of his tiger skin. Mohendra was extremely surprised and very angry indeed.

Seeing him Nabinananda laughed and said. "How is it, Gossain? How can there be so much mistrust between two Santans?"

Mohendra said, "Was Bhavananda Thakur trustworthy?"

Nabinananda rolled his eyes and said, "Did Kalyani ever touch Bhavananda and untie his tiger-skin?" Saying this Santi held back Kalyani's hands, she did not let her untie the tiger-skin.

Mohendra: What then?

Nabinananda: You may mistrust me, how can you lose faith in Kalyani?

Mohendra now felt nonplussed. He asked, "Why? How did I mistrust her?"

Nabinananda: Why did you then follow me like this into the inner precincts of the house?

Mohendra: I had something to say to Kalyani, so I came.

Nabinananda: Then please go now. I also have got something to say to Kalyani. You go out now, let me talk first. It is your own house, you are free to come whenever you like, I have come once with great difficulty.

Mohendra stood there quite at his wits end. He could non understand anything. They did not at all talk or look like culprits. Kalyani's behaviour was also strange. She too did not run away like a faithless woman, nor did she seem to be afraid or ashamed, she rather stood there smiling. Besides the same Kalyani who so easily could swallow poison under that tree, could she be faithless? Mohendra was thinking in this strain when unfortunately Santi, seeing Mohendra's plight smiled and darted at Kalyani a glamourous glance. Suddenly the darkness lifted. Mohendra could clearly recognise the glance to be that of a woman. Taking up courage he pulled at Nabinananda's beard with both his hands. The false-beard came off. Taking that opportunity Kalyani untied the knot of the tiger-skin, that too came off and fell down. Caught like this Santi hung her head down.

Mohendra then asked her. "Who are you?"

Santi: Sreeman Nabinananda Goswami.

Mohendra: That is all false play. You are a woman.

Santi: Now necessarily so.

Mohendra: Then let me ask you one question, being a woman why do you live with Jivananda Thakur?

Santi: I need not explain that to you.

Mohendra: Does Jivananda Thakur know that you are a woman?

Santi: Yes, he knows it quite well.

Hearing this pure-hearted Mohendra became sad and depressed.

Seeing this Kalyani could not help saying, "She is Santi Devi, the wedded wife of Jivananda Goswami."

Just for a moment Mohendra's face cleared. Again it became clouded. Kalyani understood everything and added, "She is a Brahmacharini."

Chapter IV

NORTH Bengal became free from the grip of the Mohammedans; but none of the Mussulmans admitted it, they deluded themselves and gave out, publicly, "A few dacoits are creating mischief there, we are punishing them." None could say how long this state of things would have continued. But just then by the grace of Providence Warren Hastings became the Governor-General in Calcutta. He was not a man to hood-wink himself and remain satisfied; had he that trait in his character where would British Empire in India be today? So without delay a new military leader Major Edwards came with a new army to conquer the bands of Santans.

Edwards understood quite well, that, this was not a war in the European sense. The enemies had no regular army, no city or capital of their own, no particular fort, yet everything was virtually under them. Wherever the British regiment encamped for the day, that part of the country came under their sway for that day. Directly the force struck their tents and marched away, "Hail Mother" began to be sung everywhere. The Sahib could not find out, wherefrom like swarms of ants the Santans came out, burnt down the village which had submitted to the British or cut down small parties of the British force wherever they met them. From continued enquiry he found out, that, these people had built a fort in the village of Padachinha and were now guarding their treasury and arsenal there. So he thought it expedient to occupy this fort.

He began to collect information about the exact number of Santans living at Padachinha. After the information he received he did not consider it wise to attack the fort. He matured a fine strategy for the purpose.

The full-moon festival of the month of Magh was near at hand. There was a fair to be held near his encampment on the river side. This year particularly the fair will be on a grander scale. Usually lacs of men gather here on this occasion. As this year the Vaishnavas had become the ruler of the land they decided to join the fair in force in order to show off their pride. So there is just a possibility that all the Santans will gather in that fair on full-moon day. Major Edwards thought that guards entrusted with the defence of Padachinha also may visit the fair. He would then march on Padachinha and occupy it.

Deciding thus the Major gave out that he would attack the fair; he would get all the Vaishnavas gathered at one place and in this way he would wipe out all his enemies, he would not allow the fair to be held.

This news was allowed to spread from village to village. Anybody who belonged to the Santan sect anywhere took up arms and rushed to defend the fair. All the Santans assembled on the riverside on the full-moon day in the month of Magh. Whatever the Major had thought out materialised. Fortunately for the British Mohendra also stepped into this trap. Keeping a handful of men to guard Padachinha Mohendra started for the fair taking the bulk of the fighters under him.

Before all this happened Santi and Jivananda had gone out of Padachinha. There was no talk of fighting then, there heart was not in it They had decided to expiate for the sin of breaking their vows by drowning themselves on the sacred full-moon day of the month of Magh at a very auspicious moment. On the way they heard that there would be a big battle between the British and the Santans assembled in the Fair. Jivananda said, "Let us then die in battle, come on quick."

They proceeded fast. The road passed over a mound at one Particular place. Climbing the mound the heroic couple found the British tamped at some distance below them. Santi said, "Don't talk about dying now, shout, — "Hail Mother!"

Chapter V

THEN both of them consulted together in whispers. After consultation Jivananda hid himself in a forest. Santi entered a different forest and began to behave in a strange manner.

Santi was going to die, she had decided to dress in feminine apparel at the time of her death. Mohendra had declared her man's guise to be a false trick. It was no use dying in false colours. So she had brought her basket containing feminine nick-nacks with her. All her apparels and articles were there. Nabinananda now opened her basket and began changing her dress.

She painted her face putting a pretty sepia spot between the eye-brows; she half covered her moon like face with pretty curls as was the fashion at that time and then in the dress of a Vaishnabi with a Sarang in her hand she made her appearance in the British Camp. Seeing her the Sepahis with beards of the colour of a jet black bumblebee became enamoured and excited. Some ordered her to sing a *Tappa* song, another a *Gazal,* a third a song about Kali, a fourth about Krishna and all had their desires satisfied. Some gave her rice, some a quantity of pulse, another sugar, and still another pice or a four anna bit. When the Vaishnabi was on the point of leaving after carefully studying the situation in the camp, the Sepahis asked her, "When are you coming again?" The Vaishnabi said, "I don't know when that will be. My home is far off from here." The Sepahis enquired, "How far?" The Vaishnabi said, "I live at Padachinha." On that very day the Major Sahib was making enquiries about Padachinha; one of the Sipahis knew that. He took the Vaishnabi to the Captain. He took her to the Major. The Vaishnabi smiled sweetly, enamoured the Major with a piercingly glamorous glance, then striking her cymbals together she sang —

Sahib asked her, "Where do you live *Bibi*?"

The *Bibi* answered, "I am not a *Bibi,* I am a Vaishnabi. My home is at Padachinha."

Sahib: Where is that Adsin padsin? Is there a *gar* (meaning a fort) there?

Vaishnabi: *Ghar?* O yes, there are any number of *ghars* (meaning rooms).

Sahib: O, no, not *ghar,* but *gar.*

Sahib: I understand what you are driving at. You mean a fort?

Sahib: Yes, a *Gar,* a *Gar* — that's what I mean. Is there one?

Santi: Yes, there is a fort, a very big fort indeed.

Sahib: How many men are there in that fort?

Santi: How many stay there? Twenty to fifty thousands.

Sahib: Nonsense! There can be only two to four thousands in one fort. Are they all there? Or they have left?

Santi: Where will they go?

Sahib: To the fair? — When did you leave the place?

Santi: I left yesterday, Sahib.

Sahib: They may have left the fort by this time.

Santi was thinking mentally, "If I don't cook the dinner for your burial service, I paint my face in vain. When will the jackals eat your head and I shall have the pleasure to witness it?" Aloud she said, "Sahib, it may be what you say; they may have left today. I don't know such details. I am only a Vaishnabi and earn my living by singing from door to door. I don't care to know such particulars. My throat is sore with talking, come, let me have my tip and go. Make the tip worth it, I shall come day after tomorrow and bring information."

Sahib threw down a rupee and said, "Bibi, not day after tomorrow please."

Santi: For shame, you blessed mother's son! Call me Vaishnabi, not *Bibi.*

Edwards: Not day after, tonight I must have the news.

Santi: You lay your head on the butt of your gun and with mustard oil in your nostrils go to sleep. I shall go twenty miles and come back again twenty miles on foot! *Chhuncho-beta.* (You son of a rat.)

Sahib: What is a *chhuncho-beta*?

Santi: It means a hero, a big general.

Edwards: I may become a great general like Clive. But I must have the information today. I shall give you a reward of rupees hundred.

Santi: You may give me hundred or even up to a thousand. But my two poor legs will not be able to cover forty miles.

Edwards: On horse back?

Santi: If I knew how to ride a horse why should I come and beg in your camp with a Sarang?

Edwards: You will ride pillion with me.

Santi: I shall ride pillion with you? Do you think I am shameless?

Edwards: What a bother! I shall give you five hundred rupees.

Sahib: Who will go, you yourself?

The Sahib then pointed out a young ensign Mr. Lindley standing in front of him and asked him, "Lindley, will you go?" Enamoured with Santi's youth and beauty he answered, "Most gladly."

A big Arabian horse was got ready and Lindley made preparations to start. He wanted to pick up Santi and put her on the horse. Santi remonstrated, "For shame! In the presence of so many people? Do you think I have no shame? Let us get out of the camp."

Lindley got upon the horse and went on at a slow pace. Santi followed him on foot. In this manner they left the camp.

Reaching a lonely field outside the British camp Santi put her foot on Lindley's foot and in one leap vaulted on the horse. Lindley laughed and said, "You seem to be a trained rider."

Santi said, "We are so well-trained that I feel ashamed to ride with you. Fie! It is silly to ride with the help of stirrups."

Just to show off his cleverness Lindley removed his foot from the stirrup. Immediately Santi gripped his neck and threw down the foolish Englishman. Then Santi seating herself properly on horse-back struck the side of the horse with her ankles and set the Arabian horse at full gallop. For four years continually living and moving with the Santan army Santi had learnt riding very well indeed. Could she live with Jivananda unless she did all that? Lindley lay there with his legs fractured. Santi rode away like the very winds.

Santi went to the forest where Jivananda was in hiding and acquainted him with all these facts. Jivananda said, "Then let me go and warn Mahehdra. You go to the fair and inform Satyananda. You go on horse-back, so that our Master may get the news quickly." Then the two rushed away different ways. It is needless to say, Santi again put on the garb of Nabinananda.

Chapter VI

EDWARDS was a clever resourceful Englishman. He had his men placed at every outpost. Very soon news was brought to him, that, the Vaishnabi having thrown Lindley down had ridden away somewhere on horseback. Hearing this Edwards said, "An imp of Satan! Strike the tents."

Then the pegs everywhere began to be struck with mallets with clatter and din. The city of tents disappeared like a heavenly city built with clouds. Goods were loaded on carts and men were disposed off on horseback or on foot. Hindus, Mohammedans, Madrasis and Britishers marched with crunching boots and with guns on their shoulders. The gun carriages rolled on noisily.

On the other side Mohendra approached the fair with his hordes of Santan force. That evening Mohendra thought, "The day is nearing its close, let us camp somewhere."

It was considered wise then to encamp at a suitable spot. The Vaishnabas had no tent. They slept under trees spreading their gunny pieces on the ground. They spent the night drinking water offered at the feet of Hari. What hunger was left unappeased was satisfied in dream drinking nectar from the lips of their Vaishnabis. There was a spot in the neighbourhood ideal for encamping. It was a big garden full of mango, jackfruit, *babla* and tamarind trees. Mohendra ordered his men, "Encamp here." There was a mound by its side, rough and uneaven to ascend. The idea once crossed Mohendra's mind, that, it would be good to camp on the top of that hillock. He decided to go and investigate.

Thinking thus Mohendra slowly ascended the mound on horseback. When he had gone up part of the way, a young Vaishnava entered the ranks of the fighters and said, "Come, let us climb on the mound." They were all surprised and asked, "Why?"

The young warrior stood upon a small mound of earth and cried, "Come on! On this moonlit night inhaling the fresh fragrance of the new spring-time flowers we will have to fight with our enemies. The soldiers all recognised the young warrior to be their general Jivananda. Then shouting the battle cry, "O Hari! O Murari!" the entire Santan army raised themselves erect with their lances and imitating Jivananda began rushing up in a body towards the top of the hillock. Someone brought a caparisoned horse to Jivananda. Mohendra noticed this from a distance and stood there in surprise. He thought, "What is this? Why are they coming up without orders?"

Thinking thus Mohendra whipping his horse began rushing down in a cloud of dust. Having met Jivananda in the forefront of the force he asked, "What is this, Ananda (delight)?"

Jivananda laughed and said, "Today is a day of great rejoicing. Edwards is on the other side of the mound. Whoever climbs on the top first wins."

Then Jivananda shouted to the Santans, "You know me? I am Jivananda Goswami. I have killed a thousand enemies."

With a great din resounding the fields and the forest they cried back in answer, "We know you, you are Jivananda Goswami.

Jivananda: Say — "O Hari! O Murari!"

From thousands of throats rose the answering cry — "O Hari! O Murari!"

Jivananda: The enemies are on the other side of the hillock. Today on this hillock the Santans will join battle the witness of which will be the blue dome above and the night below. Come, quick, whoever reaches the top first wins.

Say — "Hail Mother!"

Then both the field and the forest reverberated with the song — "Hail Mother." Slowly the Santan army began to climb the hillock. But they suddenly saw in alarm that Mohendra Singha was rushing down the mound sounding his whistle. In a very short time against the blue sky on the top of the hillock British guns with gunners were visible. In loud voice the Vaishnab army sang —

> Thou art wisdom, thou art law,
> Thou art heart — our soul — our breath,

Thou the love divine — the awe
In our hearts that conquers death.

But the loud report of the British cannons drowned that noble song. Hundreds of Santans fell down dead and dying on the mound with their arms clutched. Again mocking the bones of *Dadhichi,*[1] and taunting the waves of the sea the thunders of the British guns began rolling. The Santan army began to fall cut into pieces like ripe paddy before a scythe. In vain Jivananda toiled and Mohendra took such pains. Like a falling shower of stones the Santan army turned and descended down the hillock. They fled hither and thither at random. Then in order to wipe out the entire force the British soldiers began descending with the cry — "Hurrah! Hurrah!" With raised bayonets like a vast and loosened hill-torrent the countless unconquerable and fierce British soldiers began chasing the fleeing Santans. Jivananda meeting Mohendra once said, "Today is the end of everything. Come, let us die here."

Mohendra said, "If dying meant winning battle I would gladly die. To die in vain is not the religion of a hero."

Jivananda: I shall die in vain, even then I shall have the consolation of dying in battle.

Then turning back Jivananda cried aloud, "Whoever prefers to die with the name of Hari on his lips, come with me!"

Many came forward. Jivananda said, "No, not like that. Take a vow before Hari that you will not return alive."

Those who had come forward fell back. Jivananda said, "No one will come it seems. Then let me go forward alone."

Jivananda raised himself on horseback and called out to Mohendra who was far behind, "Brother, tell Nabinananda that I have gone, we shall meet in heaven."

Then that heroic figure dashed his horse in that hail of bullets, his left

---

[1]Dadhichi is primarily known for sacrificing his life so the Gods could make weapons called "Vajra" from his bones. After being driven out from *Svarga*, or heaven, by the serpent king *Vritra*, the Deva defeated the *Asura* by using their vajra to reclaim heaven. He is well known for his sacrifice, in spite of his wife's crying for that he convinced her stating that.

hand holding the lance, the right hand the gun, his lips crying "Hare Murare! Hare Murare! Hare Murare!" There was hardly any chance of a fight. There was no meaning in this courage. Even then Jivananda crying "Hare Murare! Hare Murare!" entered the serried ranks of the foe.

Mohendra called the fleeing Santans — "Turn once and look at Jivananda Gosain. Looking back once will not mean death for you."

Turning back some of them saw Jivananda's superhuman feat. At first they were amazed, then they said, "Only Jivananda knows how to die, we don't know? Come, let us follow Jivananda to Heaven."

Hearing this some Santans turned back; their example made others turn, theirs again still others. A great uproar set in. Jivananda had already entered the ranks of the enemy. No one could find him.

In the meantime from all over the battle field fleeing Santans began detecting that parties of Santans were turning back. All came to the conclusion that the Santans were victorious. They were chasing the enemy. Then the whole body of Santans cried out "Kill! Kill!" and rushed at the British.

On the other side there was a great confusion created among the British force. The Sipahis without caring for fight were fleeing right and left, the white soldiers were also turning back to their camp with raised bayonets. Looking about intently Mohendra found innumerable Santans on the creep of the hillock. They were heroically descending the hillock and attacking the British force. Then he called back his men and said, "Look! There is our Master Satyananda's flag visible on the top. Today Murari himself, the killer of Madhu and Kaitava, the destroyer of Kansa and Kesi has come down to join the fray. One hundred thousand Santans are on the hillock. Say, "Hare Murare! Hare Murare!" Get upon the back and the chest of the Musalmans and strangle them. There are a hundred thousand Santans on the rock."

Then the cry of "Hare Murare" echoed through the field and the forest. The Santans' cry of, "No fear! No fear!" and the sweet music of clashing weapons entranced every living creature. The army of Mohendra began rushing up mightily. Like the current of a stream sent back and broken up dashing against a stone barrier the government army became stunned and panic-stricken and utterly broken. Just at that moment Satyananda Brahmachari with his twenty-five thousand troops fell upon them from the crest of the hillock like a mighty sea wave. A great battle was fought there.

Just as a small fly is crushed between two big stones, so the huge government army was crushed between the two bodies of Santans.

There was no one left alive to carry the news to Warren Hastings.

Chapter VII

IT WAS a full-moon night. That awesome battle-field was quiet. The clatter of horses' hoofs, the rattle of muskets, the booming of guns and that spreading pall of smoke — all were gone. Nobody was crying "Hurrah" now, none shouting "Hari! Hari!" All the noise that was made there was coming from jackals, dogs and vultures. Above all there was the fitful moaning of the wounded. Some of them had their hands torn away, some with broken heads, some with their legs fractured and others had their ribs pierced. A few of them were crying out, "O father!" Some of them asked for water, some wanted escape from pain through death. Bengalis, Hindustanis, Englishmen, Mussulmans all lay promiscuously intertwined. The living and the dead, men and horses were lying closely packed, mixed up and pressed together. The battle-field was looking horrible in that intensely cold full-moon night in month of Magh. No one had the nerve to go there.

Though nobody dared, yet that night a woman was moving about in that unapproachable battle-field. With a burning torch she was looking for something among the dead bodies. She was approaching every corpse and looking at its face with her lighted torch, and then was moving on to another on a similar errand. At one spot a human body was covered under a dead horse, there the young woman putting down her torch on the ground rescued the dead one by removing the horse with both her hands. Then when she found that the person was not the one she was looking for, she moved away with her torch. Searching thus the young woman went through all the fields, but nowhere could she find; what she sought for. Then throwing away her torch she began rolling and writhing in the agony of grief on that bloody ground full of the dead and wept. She was Santi looking for Jivananda's body.

Santi cried in utter despair. Just then a very sweet and voice entered her ear. As if some one was saying, "Mother, get up; don't weep." Santi looked up and saw a tall and superhuman figure with matted locks standing in front of her in that moon light.

Santi got up. The one who had come said to her, "Don't weep

mother! I shall find out Jivananda's body for you, come with me."

Then that saintly man took Santi to the very heart and centre of that battle-field. There innumerable corpses were lying in a huddled heap. Santi had not been able to move them all aside. Removing all those bodies that massive and powerfully built person picked out and recovered a certain corpse. Santi could recognise that one to be Jivananda's body. It was covered all over with wounds and smeared with blood. Santi wept aloud like an ordinary woman.

Again the saintly man said, "Don't weep, mother! Is Jivananda really dead? Be calm and examine his body. First feel his pulse."

Santi felt the pulse. There was not the slightest movement there. The saint said, "Feel his chest with your hand."

Santi put her hand where the heart was, there was not a sign of life. It was quite cold.

The Saint again said, "Put your hand near his nose — is there any breath moving?"

Santi examined the body as directed, but could not find sign of any breath.

He said, "Try again, feel inside his mouth with your finger, whether there is any warmth there."

Santi felt with her finger and said, "I can't feel anything." Hope was acting like wine in her.

The great Saint touched the body of Jivananda with his left hand. He said, "Fear has robbed you of all hope, so you cannot feel anything.

There is a little warmth left still in the body. Feel again."

Santi then felt the pulse again, there was some throbbing there. Surprised, Santi put her hand on his heart — it was beating slightly. She held her finger before the nostrils, there was indeed some breath going. She felt a little warmth too in his mouth. Amazed Santi asked, "Was there life in him indeed, or it has returned?"

The Saint said, "How can that be possible, mother? Will you be able to carry him to the tank? I am a doctor, I shall treat him."

Santi picked up Jivananda's body with perfect ease and began carrying him towards the tank. The doctor said, "You take him to the pond and wash his wounds. I shall go and fetch medicine."

Santi took Jivananda to the side of the tank and washed his wounds. Soon after the doctor brought some crushed wild herbs and applied them to all his wounds. Then he passed his hands again and again on Jivananda's body. After inhaling deeply Jivananda sat up. He looking at Santi asked, "Which side has become victorious?"

Santi said, "You have conquered. Bow dawn to this great Saint."

Then both of them found that there was no one there. To whom was he to bow down!

The uproar of the victorious Santan army could be heard from the neighbourhood. But neither, Santi nor Jivananda stirred. They went on sitting on that moonlit steps of the tank. In a very short time Jivananda's wounds were healed. He said, "Santi, the herbs of that doctor has wonderful healing properties. There is hardly any pain or trouble left in my body. Come, let us now depart wherever you wish. There comes the cry of jubilation of the Santans."

Santi said. "We need not go there anymore. The Mother's work is done. This country belongs to the Santans. We don't crave for any share in this government, then where is the good of going there?"

Jivananda: What we have taken by force must be protected by the prowess of our arms.

Santi: To protect it there is Mohendra, Satyenanda himself is there. As an act of expiation for the sake of the Santan religion you gave up your body. The Santans have no claim on this rejuvenated body. So far as they are concerned we are dead. Now if they see us the Santans will say, "Jivananda had hid himself for fear of expiation, now finding the Santans victorious he has come forward to take his share of the newly won kingdom."

Jivananda: How do you mean, Santi? Shall I shirk my duty for fear of blame? My duty is the service of the Mother. Whatever others may say, I must go on serving her.

Santi: You have no longer the right to serve the Mother, because in her service you have given up this body. Where is your expiation if you get a fresh opportunity to serve the Mother? The chief part of this expiation is to be deprived of the pleasure of serving her. Only to give up your trifling body is neither very difficult nor enough for the purpose.

Jivananda: Santi, you always get the right perspective. I won't leave my expiation incomplete; my chief pleasure is in the Santan religion. I shall deprive myself of that. But where shall I go? Giving up service of the Mother I cannot go home and enjoy myself.

Santi: Am I telling you to do that? We are no more householders. We shall continue to remain Sannyasis like this — we shall go on practising celibacy. Come, let us travel all over the country on pilgrimage.

Jivananda: And then after that?

Santi: Then we shall build a cottage on the Himalayas and worship God there — seeking from him the boon of the Mother's complete wellbeing.

Then both of them got up, clasped each other's hand and disappeared in that moonlit night.

O Mother! Will you come again? Will you bear in your womb sons like Jivananda and daughters like Santi?

Chapter VIII

SATYANANDA Thakur left the battle-field without telling anything to anybody and came to Anandamath. There on the court-yard of the Vishnu temple at dead of night he sat in deep meditation. Just then that doctor made his appearance there. Seeing him Satyananda got up and made his obeisance to him.

The doctor said, "Satyananda, to-day is the full-moon night of the month of Magh."

Satyananda: Let us go, I am ready. But O Noble hearted one! deign to remove a certain doubt from my mind. At the very moment when I have succeeded in making the Santan religion safe through war, why do you come and recall me?

He who had come said, "Your work is accomplished, the Mussulman kingdom is destroyed. You have no other work now. Further slaughter of living creatures is useless."

Satyananda: The Mussulman domination is done away with but no Hindu kingdom has yet been established. The English are strong in Calcutta now.

He said, "The Hindu kingdom is not destined yet to be established. Your presence here will mean useless loss of human life. So come away with me."

Hearing this Satyananda felt acutely distressed. He said, "My Master! If the Hindu kingdom will not be established, then who will rule here? Will the Mussulman again get the upper hand?"

He said, "No, the English will rule India now."

Tears flowed from both of Satyananda's eyes. Turning towards the image of Mother India placed on high, he began saying in tear-choked voice with joined plams, "Alas Mother! I have failed to rescue you, you will again fall into the clutches of the *Mlechhas* (Non-Aryans). Do condone the failing of your child. Alas Mother! Why did I not die in the battle-field today?"

The doctor said, "Satyananda, don't be broken-hearted. Due to your error of judgment you gathered money through robbery and thus won the war. Out of sin does not come pure achievement. So you will necessarily fail to rescue your country. Moreover, whatever will happen will be for the best. Unless the English rule this land, there is no chance of the renaissance of the eternal religion. Listen patiently. I shall explain to you as it has been seen and understood by the ancient sages. The worship of three hundred and thirty million deities is not the eternal religion; that is an inferior popular religion. Under its influence, the true religion, as the *Mlechhas* call it, is lost. The true Hindu religion is based on knowledge, not on action. That knowledge is of two kinds; — secular or external and spiritual or internal. The inner spiritual knowledge is the chief part of true religion. But unless secular knowledge about the outside world comes the other knowledge about the inner world cannot grow. Unless one knows what the gross is, one cannot arrive at the knowledge pertaining to the subtle. For a long time this esoteric knowledge has been lost in this country — so the true eternal religion is also lost. In order to restore the eternal religion, at the outset knowledge of the material world must be preached. There is not much material knowledge in the country now, there is none capable of teaching it. We are not adepts in spreading popular education. So the necessary knowledge has got to be brought and introduced from other countries. The English are past masters in the knowledge pertaining to the material world. They are adepts in the art of teaching. So we shall make the British our rulers. Through English education our people attaining knowledge of the material world will also be made capable of understanding inner knowledge. There will then be no obstacle against preaching the true eternal religion. True religion will, under the circumstances, grow spontaneously. So long as that does not happen, so long as the Hindus do not become wise, worthy and strong, British rule will endure. The subjects will be happy under the British control. They will pursue their religious life without hindrance. So, O wise one! Desist from fighting the British and follow me."

Satyananda said, "O noble-hearted one! If our purpose was to put the British in control over us as our rulers, if British rule was considered beneficent for our country, then why did you engage us in this heartless fighting?"

The Saint said, "The English are now merchants, they are busy earning money, they do not care to undertake the responsibility of government. Under the pressure of this Santan rebellion they will be compelled to undertake the responsibility of governing this country. Because without that the financial resources of the country cannot be explored. The Santan rebellion has come only to put the British on the throne. Come now with me, you will understand things yourself after attaining knowledge."

Satyananda: O Noble-hearted one! I don't crave after knowledge, I have no use for it. I shall fulfil the vow that I have taken. Bless me so that my devotion to my Mother remains unshakable.

The Sage: Your vow stands fulfilled — you have achieved the well-being of your Mother — you have helped to establish British Rule. Give up fighting, let people engage in cultivation, let the earth become fruitful with crops, let the people of the country become prosperous." As if sparks flew from Satyananda's eyes. He said, "I shall drench the mother earth with the enemy's blood and thus make her fruitful."

The Sage: Who is your enemy? Here is hardly any enemy. The British are our ally and friendly power. Besides none has the requisite power to be victorious in the long run in a war against the British.

Satyananda: If we haven't got the power, I shall give up my body before this image of my Motherland.

The Sage: You will die in ignorance? Come, attain knowledge first. There is the Mother's temple on the peak of the Himalayas, from there I shall reveal and show you her true form.

Saying this the sage grasped Satyananda's hand. How sublime! In that magnificent Vishnu temple before the huge four-handed image in dim light stood the two great personalities — talent and genius incarnate — one holding the hand of the other. Who has gripped whom? Knowledge stands wedded to devotion — religion has embraced Karma or action — renunciation is coupled with success — Kalyani has grasped the hand of Santi. This Satyananda is Santi; this Sage is Kalyani. Satyananda is success, and this Saint stands for renunciation.

Renunciation came and took success away.

Appendices

I
HISTORY OF THE SANNYASI REBELLION FROM WARREN HASTINGS' LETTER IN GLEIG'S MEMOIRS

You will hear of great disturbances committed by the Sannyasis or wandering Fakeers who annually infest the provinces, about this time of the year in pilgrimages to Jaggarnaut, going in bodies of 1,000 and sometimes even 10,000 men. An officer of reputation (Captain Thomas) lost his life in an unequal attack upon a party of these banditti, about 3,000 of them, near Rungpoor with a small party of Purgunnah Sepoys, which has made them more talked of than they deserve. The revenue, however, has felt the effects of their ravages in the northern districts. The new establishment of Sepoys which is now forming on the plan enjoined by the Court of Directors and the distribution of them ordered for the internal protection of the provinces, will, I hope, effectually secure them hereafter from these incursions.

(Hastings to Sir George Colebrooke
2 February 1773
Gleig's Memoirs Vol. I.)

* * *

Our own province has worn something of a warlike appearance, this year, having been infested by bands of Sannyasis, who have defeated two small parties of Purgunnah Sepoys (a rascally corps) and cut off the two officers who commanded them. One was Captain Thomas whom you knew. Four battalions of the brigade Sepoys are now in pursuit of them, but they will not stand an engagement and have neither camp equipage, nor even clothes to retard their flight. Yet I hope we shall yet make an example of some of them as they are shut in by the rivers which they cannot pass when closely pursued.

The history of this people is curious. They inhabit or rather possess the country lying south of the hills of Tibet from Kabul to China. They go mostly naked, they have neither towns, houses, nor families, but rove continually from place to place recruiting their numbers with the healthiest children they can steal in the countries through which they pass. Thus they are the stoutest and the most active men in India. Many are merchants. They are all pilgrims and held by all castes of Gentoos in great veneration. This infatuation prevents our obtaining any intelligence of their motions or aid from the country against them, notwithstanding very rigid orders which have been published for these purposes, in so much that they often appear in the heart of the province as if they dropped from heaven. They are hardy, bold and enthusiastic to a degree surpassing credit. Such are the Sannyasis, the gipsies of Hindusthan.

We have dissolved all the Purgunnah Sepoys and fixed stations of the brigade Sepoys on our frontiers, which are to be employed only in the defence of the provinces, and to be relieved every three months. This I hope will secure the peace of the country against future irruptions, and as they are no longer to be employed in the collections, the people will be freed from the oppressions of our own plunderers.

(Hastings to Josiss Du Pre
9 March, 1773)

* * *

We have lately been much troubled here with hordes of disparate adventurers called Sannyasis, who have overrun the province in great numbers and committed great depredations. The particulars of these disturbances and of our endeavours to repel them you will find in our general letters and consultations, which will acquit the Government of any degree of blame from such a calamity. At this time we have five battalions of Sepoys in pursuit of them, and I have still hopes of exacting ample vengeance for the mischief they have done us as they have no advantage over us, but in the speed with which they fly from us. A minute relation of these adventures cannot amuse you, nor indeed are they of great moment, for which reason give me leave to drop the subject, and lead you to one in which you cannot but be most interested, etc.

(Hastings to Purling
31 March, 1772
Gleig's Memoirs of Hastings — Vol. I.)

* * *

In my last I mentioned that we had every reason to suppose the Sannyasi Fakeers had entirely evacuated the Company's possessions. Such were the advices I then received, and their usual progress made this highly probable. But it seems they were either disappointed in crossing the Burramputrah river, or they changed intention, and returned in several bands of about 2,000 or 3,000 each, appearing unexpectedly in different parts of the Rungpoor and Dinagpoor provinces. For in spite of the strictest orders issued and the severest penalties threatened to the inhabitants in case they fail in giving intelligence of the approach of the Sannyasis, they are so infatuated by superstition as to be backward in giving the information, so that the banditti are sometimes advanced into the very heart of our province before we know anything of their motions; as if they dropped from heaven to punish the inhabitants for their folly. One of these parties falling in with a small detachment commanded by Captain Edwards, an engagement ensued wherein our Sepoys gave way. Captain Edwards lost his life in endeavouring to cross a Nullah. This detachment was formed of the very worst of our Purgunnah Sepoys, who seemed to have behaved very ill. This success elated the Sannyasis, and I heard of their depredations from every quarter in those districts. Captain Stewart, with the nineteenth battalion of Sepoys, who was before employed against them, was vigilant in the pursuit wherever he could hear of them, but to no purpose. They were gone before he could reach the places to which he was directed. I ordered another battalion from Burrampoor to march immediately to co-operate with Captain Stewart, but to act separately in order to have the better chance of falling in with them. At the same time I ordered another battalion to march from the Dinapoor station through Tyroot and by the northern frontier of the

Purnea province, following the track which the Sannyasis usually took, in order to intercept them in case they marched that way. This battalion after acting against the Sannyasis, if occasion offered, was directed to pursue their march to Cooch Baher, where they are to join Captain Jones and assist in the reduction of that country.

Several parties of the Sannyasis having entered into the Purnea province burning and destroying many villages there, collector applied to Captain Brook, who had just arrived at Panity near Rajmahal, with his newly raised battalion of light infantry. That officer immediately crossed the river and entered upon measures against the Sannyasis and had very near fallen in with a party of them, just as they were crossing the Cosa river, to escape out of that province. He arrived on the opposite bank before their rear had entirely crossed; but too late to do any execution among them. It is apparent now that the Sannyasis are glad to escape as fast as they can out off the Company's possessions, but I am still in hopes, that some of the many detachments now acting against them may fall in with some of their parties, and punish them exemplarily for their audacity.

It is impossible but that on account of the various depredations which the Sannyasis have committed, the revenue must fall short in some of the Company's districts as well from real as from pretended losses. The Board of Revenue, aware of this last consideration, have come to the resolution of admitting no pleas for a reduction of revenue but such as are attended with circumstances of conviction and by this means they hope to prevent, as much as in their power, all impositions on the Government, and to render the loss to the Company as inconsiderable as possible. Effectual means will be used by stationing some small detachments at proper posts on our frontier to prevent any future incursions from the Sannyasi Fakeers, or any other roving banditti, a measure which only the extraordinary audacity of their last incursions hath manifested to be necessary. This will be effected without employing many troops, and I hope that in no future time the revenues shall again suffer from this cause.

(Hastings to Sir George Colebrooke
3 March, 1773)

* * *

The Sannyasis threatened us with the same disturbances from the beginning of this year as we experienced from them the last. But by being early provided to oppose them, and one or two severe checks which they received in their first attempts, we have kept the country clear of them. A party of horse, which we employed in pursuit of them, has chiefly contributed to intimidate these ravagers, who seemed to pay little regard to our Sepoys, having so much the advantage of them in speed, on which they entirely rely for their safety. It is my intention to proceed more effectually against them by expelling them from their fixed residences which they have established in the north-eastern quarter of the province, and by making severe examples of the zemindars, who have afforded them protection, or assistance.

(Hastings to Laurence Sulivan
20 March, 1774.)

II
HISTORY OF THE SANNYASI REBELLION FROM THE ANNALS OF RURAL BENGAL

"A set of lawless banditti," wrote the Council, in 1773, "known under the name of Sannyasis or Fakeers, have long infested these countries and under pretence of religious pilgrimage, have been accustomed to traverse the chief part of Bengal, begging, stealing, and plundering wherever they go, and as it best suits their convenience to practise. In the years subsequent to the famine, their ranks were swollen by a crowd of starving peasants, who had neither seed nor implements to recommence cultivation with, and the cold weather of 1772 brought them down upon the harvest fields of Lower Bengal, burning, plundering, ravaging 'in bodies of fifty to thousand men.' The collectors called on the military; but after a temporary success, our Sepoys 'were at length totally defeated and Captain Thomas (their leader) with almost the whole party were cut off.' It was not till the close of the winter that the Council could report to the Court of Directors, that a battalion under an experienced commander had acted successfully against them; and a month later we find that even this tardy intimation had been premature. On the 31st March, 1773, Warren Hastings plainly acknowledges that the commander who had succeeded Captain Thomas unhappily underwent the same fate; that four battalions of the army were then actively engaged against the banditti, but that in spite of the militia levies called from the landholders their combined operations had been fruitless. The revenue could not be collected, the inhabitants made common cause with the marauders and the whole rural administration was unhinged. Such incursions were annual episodes in what some have been pleased to represent as the still life of Bengal."

(Hunter's Annals of Rural Bengal – P. 70 — 2.)